MISFIT CHRISTMAS

A COLORADO HOLIDAY ROMANCE

ANNE HAGAN

PUBLISHED BY:
Jug Run Press, USA
Copyright © 2021

https://annehaganauthor.com/

❀ Created with Vellum

1

MEET CUTE

Monday, November 11th
Sun Valley Community Recreation Center
Denver, Colorado

When she heard the popping sound, Sofia looked up from the craft project she was helping with a small group of six- and seven-year-olds with. Across the multi-purpose room, Clevon, their resident clown and want to be stand-up comedian was in the center of a circle of his peers. She couldn't see what he'd done to create the noise, but the laughter that followed seemed harmless enough to her. She let it go.

"How does this look, Miss Sofia?" a six-year-old girl asked. She held up her construction paper fall tree project.

"It's beautiful, Maya. You've done a great job."

"I don't get to see no trees like this very often."

"Many trees," Sofia gently corrected the youngster.

Maya didn't parrot back the correction like she usually did.

Instead, she laid the tree aside and asked, "What are we doing next?"

Sofia glanced around the table. "Well, first we need to clean-up all the glue mess, and then I think it's time for some more juice. What do you all think?"

A couple of the other children nodded, and Maya smiled with her gap-toothed grin. "Can we have some of those cookies we had yesterday for after-school snack time too? The chocolate ones? Those were so good!"

"We'll see." Sofia cringed internally. *There's probably not much more in the cupboards at all. If we don't get some grant money soon —*

The sounds of an argument breaking out interrupted her thoughts. She looked across the room where a wrestling match was beginning between Clevon and his usual foil, DeMarco. *Here we go again.* She jumped up and headed toward the group.

Will, the rec center director, came out of the small office area and hustled toward the knot of teens and pre-teens, too. She was happy he was still around to give her some backup.

It was chilly outside when Sofia stepped out with Clevon a few minutes later. The day had been sunny, but with little cloud cover to hold the heat in, the dusk settling in promised a frigid overnight.

"Buddy," she began, "we've talked about this. You're thirteen; three years older than him and a head taller. You've got to keep—"

"He started it, Miss Sofia. I swear. I was just talkin' and he got all mad."

"Talking?" She raised an eyebrow and gave him the no nonsense look most of the kids were familiar with from her.

"Yeah. You know how we do."

"In other words, you were cutting up?"

"Well, yeah."

"What did you say to him, specifically?"

Clevon had the good grace to hang his head a bit, but his remorse only lasted a second. "You're really going to think it was funny when you hear it."

"Try me."

He stepped back and held his arms out. "I was doing new 'yo mama's I heard, like this one, "Yo momma is so ugly even Hello Kitty said, 'Goodbye' to her," and—" He swung his arms back catching a woman who stepped around the corner of the building in the solar plexus with his left. The woman dropped to the ground, landing in a heap on her backside, her legs splayed out in front of her. She heaved for breath.

While Clevon looked on in shock, Sofia rushed to the woman's aid. "Are you all right?" When no answer came, she asked again. The woman tried to inhale deeply and ended up coughing instead.

"Clevon!"

The teenager shook off his shock and looked at her.

"Help me get her up," Sofia prompted. She addressed the woman then, really focusing on her face for the first time. As she explained they were going to help her stand, she took in her short cropped black hair worn in a spiky cut that didn't need gel to stand up and her deep brown eyes. Her slightly tan face was devoid of make-up, but her cheeks were reddening from the chill of the wind.

Sofia shivered. The woman was obviously well over thirty, but she was a stunning butch, reminding her of her one and only girlfriend a few years past. She steeled herself. *Put it out of your mind. She's out of your league and you really can't go there, anyway.*

She moved to the woman's left and hooked a hand under

one arm. Clevon got on her right side and followed his counselor's lead.

Sofia realized too late the height difference she was dealing with. Clevon was managing on his side, but the woman was easily eight inches taller or more than her own five-foot, one-inch height. Unbalanced on her left and still trying to catch her breath, she lurched into Sofia, nearly toppling them both before Clevon reeled her back upright and Sofia along with her.

When they let go of her arms, the woman tugged at her short ski jacket, then dusted her hands against the backside of her dark slacks.

Sophia tried not to stare. "I'm so sorry. He's so sorry." She shot Clevon a look as she pointed at him.

He caught the hint. "Yeah. Right. Sorry, ma'am. I was just... I didn't know you were there, and I—"

Finding her voice, she snarled at him, "You need to pay more attention to what's going on around you."

Her tone took Sofia aback. "It really was an accident," she said, defending the teen she'd been about to scold herself moments before.

The other woman tried to speak again but sputtered, coughing. Between spasms, she choked out the words, "Rec center?"

Sophia pointed at the door. "Right here."

With a curt nod of her head at the two of them, she pulled open the door and went inside.

"What you think she's wanting 'round here?" Clevon asked.

Wondering the same thing, she didn't bother to correct his grammar. *She was casually dressed, but her clothes and cowboy boots were all of high quality.*

She pushed the woman out of her mind and refocused. "Let's talk about you right now. What do you think you could have done better in there?"

.   .   .

AFTER SENDING Clevon on his way home, she re-entered the building to start clean-up and marshal the remaining children out toward home.

Inside, she didn't see their visitor, and Will's door was partially closed. The kids still hanging around were sitting quietly in a semi-circle on the floor, their usual practice during the short staffing periods that had resulted from losing the bulk of the center funding.

"Okay, everyone, if you were working on crafts at all, come back over to the table. You need to help clean up." She glanced up at the clock on the wall. "Maya, get your coat and book bag. Your mama will be here any minute."

"I'll help clean up, Miss Sofia."

Sofia smiled. The youngster was always helpful. "It's okay. You already did your share." *And your mother is not the least bit patient.*

Will came out of his office with the woman trailing behind him. He waved Sofia over as he called out, "Come here. I want you to meet someone."

She glanced that way, knowing whom she'd see. *We've already met. Badly.* As she moved toward them, she held back a sigh that was half annoyance with the other woman and half something she didn't dare put a name to.

"This is Sofia Vaca, the volunteer I was telling you about," Will said to the tall butch, "And Sofia, this is Lacie Lindly. Lacie is going to be helping us out from now... er... now, through the holidays, or so. She'll be working with you."

"Her?" Lacie asked, as she ignored Sofia's outstretched hand and stayed focused on Will.

Sofia didn't care for her tone, but she held her tongue and pulled her hand back.

"I think you misunderstood me. I've got to—"

"It will be fine," he said, interrupting the newcomer. "I'll take care of the details." He turned to Sofia, "You two talk for a minute and I'll handle the cleanup and getting the crew moving."

"Uh, okay. Thanks, Will."

She looked at Lacie and took a deep breath. "I'm not sure where to start. Are you a volunteer?"

"In a manner of speaking, yes."

Oddly put.

"I take it that's what you are?" The older woman asked.

"Now, yes. I'm in my last year of my Bachelor of Social Work at Metro. I've been working here on and off since high school though as both paid and volunteer staff."

"Pardon my prying, but why aren't you drawing at least an hourly wage?" She looked over at the group of kids cleaning the table and then the teens still sitting on the floor.

"Getting paid depends a lot on donations and on how much grant money we can get to keep us afloat. We're a non-profit, not part of the string of rec centers the city operates."

"Why doesn't Denver just take this one over too?"

Sofia suppressed a shudder. "They'd probably tear it down and then not replace it. It's a resource a lot of people in this neighborhood can't afford to be without."

"But it's run down," Lacie argued. "It can't last forever."

Sofia bristled under her glare and her tone. Her irritation came out in her voice, causing Will and a few of the older kids to look her way as she responded, "We do the best we can with what we have."

Lacie glanced over at Will, and after seeing the look on his face, she softened her stance. She reached out, took Sofia by the forearm, and tugged her a few feet more out of earshot of the kids. "Let's start over, okay? I didn't mean to come off as putting this place down. I'm sure you do a lot of good around here and

I'll do my best to do what I can to help." Her grip lessened, but she didn't let go of Sofia's arm.

"In what way, exactly?" She looked the other woman up and down again as she tugged her arm away. *She's nicely dressed, but she doesn't seem wealthy.*

"My time and my expertise, whenever I can give it."

"Expertise in what?"

"I'm a business analyst. It looks like you could use some of that around here."

Sofia moved toward the hook on the wall where her coat hung. As she pulled it on, she said, "What we could use is someone who is good with kids who can help them with homework and keep them occupied after school every day without costing us a lot of money we don't have."

"Just kids? It's not mixed community use here?"

"It used to be. We don't have much besides basketball anymore to attract older users and we close at 5:30 now. Funding."

"It keeps coming back to that, doesn't it?" When Sofia didn't answer, she asked, "Can we go somewhere and get a cup of coffee and talk more about how I can help?"

Pushy. "I Can't. I've got to help Will see the kids off and my ride will be here any minute." She looked over at Will who was shepherding the remaining children toward the door, his deep baritone cautioning them to zip up and to be careful. "It's already dark out there. Watch for ice on the sidewalks," he called out.

"Gotta love daylight savings time," Lacie said, her voice tinged with what Sofia could already sense as sarcasm coming from the other woman.

They both moved outside behind the line of kids and watched as most they trudged off to the right, toward a public housing complex. Will led two of the youngest around the corner in the direction Lacie had come from, intending to walk them within sight of their homes located further down the street.

Lacie jerked a thumb the way he'd gone. "I'm parked around the corner. Not a lot of parking around here."

"The kids don't drive, and they all live within a few blocks. Besides, it's on the bus line if that works better for you."

The older woman wrinkled her nose. "Pass. I'll figure it out. When can we talk again?"

"I'm here Monday through Friday, 2:30 to 5:30, and sometimes on Saturday afternoons."

"Every day with no pay?"

"Money isn't everything," Sofia said. She pointed out to the street where a pickup truck lurched to a stop. "That's my ride."

BRITTANY'S PICKUP was a Ford beater from another era. The body looked awful, but the truck ran well, because of the mechanical skills of Britt's boyfriend and her boyfriend's father at whose knee he continued to learn his trade.

Sofia had never given a second thought to appearances while riding around in the more rust than red colored truck with her best friend, but the look on Lacie's face when Britt stopped alongside the car parked against the curb made her feel self-conscious. She scurried forward without a backward glance.

Lacie called after her. "I normally work until 4:00 or later. I'll try to get here a little earlier tomorrow so you can show me the ropes, but no promises."

"That's fine," Sofia answered before she slammed the door behind her. To Brittany she directed, "Let's get going. Dad needs my help with the horses tonight."

"Hello to you too!"

"Sorry. It's just... Will threw something in my lap today I

wasn't expecting. Well, I'm not even sure what exactly he's passed off to me, honestly."

"Does it have anything to do with that beautiful butch woman you practically ran to get away from back there?"

She gave Britt a sidelong look. "Since when do you notice women in... you know, in that way?"

Without taking her eyes off the road as she navigated out of the old, rundown neighborhood, Britt asked, "And you didn't? Please! I know you better than that, Sofia."

"I'm not even going there. She's supposedly going to be helping the center just through the holidays. By the sounds of it, she'll hardly be around, anyway."

Brittany wasn't about to let it go. "But you admit you were attracted to her?"

"What? No! I mean, she's a nice-looking lady, but she's got to be fifteen or maybe even twenty years older than me, and anyway, you know where I am. No more relationships. School is the most important thing. That, and trying to get these kids through the holidays and give them some kind of Christmas." *Not to mention not disappointing my entire family. My mother would disown me. Family is everything.*

"Are you going to need my help with the Christmas party?"

Sofia nodded, glad for the change in subject, even if it was to one that was equally anxiety producing. "Yours, my dad's, and everyone else's I can think of. It's the only Christmas a lot of those kids will have. We have to shop for gifts and make it special without it costing much."

2

JUDGEMENT

Earlier the Same Day

Kendall Jordan, one of the administrative assistants and Lacie's only real friend at work aside from Heaven, her on again, off again girlfriend, poked her head into Lacie's cubicle. "Hey girl, Judge Hildalgo's office is on line two for you."

Lacie winced. *What does he want?* "Thanks. I'll pick up as soon as I finish this." She pretended to tap away at something on her keyboard until the other woman withdrew. *She could have just transferred the call. She doesn't need to know any more than she already does.*

She took a deep breath and punched the lighted button on her desk phone. "Lacie Lindly speaking."

"This is Officer Castro. I'm an adult probation officer with the Common Pleas Court. I'm following up with you on behalf of Judge Hildalgo."

Lacie feigned a confidence she wasn't feeling. "How can I

help you, Officer?"

"You can help yourself stay out of jail by appearing at Judge Hildalgo's office at 4:00 this afternoon."

"Is this about my community service?" she asked in a voice barely above a whisper. "Because I've done—"

"Very little of it," the officer said, finishing her sentence. "I see only forty hours in your file."

I could have sworn there was a little more than that. "I'm at work. I might not be able to get there by 4:00."

"I suggest you do your best, Ms. Lindly. Don't keep the judge waiting."

She hung up, stood and left her cubicle, headed toward the ladies' room.

Kendall spotted her and followed. The other woman had the good grace to check the room to see if it was empty before confronting Lacie. "Was that about what I think it was?"

Lacie braced her hands against the long vanity and stared at her reflection. "About my community service, yes."

"Why? I thought you completed that."

I wish now that I had. "Actually, no. I have at least a few more hours. The judge wants to see me about it." She felt bad about lying to her friend, but her embarrassment trumped her feelings of guilt.

"At the courthouse?"

"In his chambers, at 4:00. I'm going to have to head out pretty soon." She thought about something else. "I told Heaven I'd meet her at Tamayo at 6:00. If she comes looking for me—"

"Kind of an expensive place for Mexican food, but it's fantastic." Kendall's mind was always on her stomach.

It's all about the view. "Her idea, not mine. You know me." She gave her friend a pained grin. "Saving all my money for a rainy day."

"Special occasion, then?"

"Not that I'm aware of." *Heaven just always wants the best of everything.* "Listen, if she asks, tell her I'll meet her there."

"She's all wrong for you, you realize that, don't you?"

"You've mentioned that." Lacie shrugged and said, "But the sex is fantastic."

"When it goes bad, you'll regret dating someone you work with. Trust me on that."

"I wouldn't call our... relationship... dating."

"Oh? What does Heaven call it?"

I really don't know. Probably don't want to. She was saved from answering Kendall's probe by another woman entering the restroom.

"THIS ISN'T A LAUGHING MATTER, Miss Lindly," Judge Hildalgo said.

Lacie wiped the smirk off her face. "I did forty hours over the summer, Your Honor." *And you sentenced me pretty harshly for such a minor first offense.* She thought about it, but she didn't dare say it. He didn't look like he was in a negotiating mood.

"You still owe the court 160 hours. Because I'm feeling benevolent today, I'm going to help you out."

She raised her eyebrows. *Maybe he is, after all.* "You're going to wipe out the rest of my time?"

Hildalgo laughed out loud. "Not hardly, Miss Lindly." He plucked a business card off his desk blotter and held it out to her.

She glanced at it. "The Sun Valley Community Recreation Center?"

"Report to Will Ellison over there. You'll do the rest of your time there and you'll do it by the end of the year."

Her face fell. "That's impossible. It's... it's November 11th. I have a job. That's... " She did some quick math, "That's almost thirty hours a week."

"You have several weekends between now and then."

"I have plans over the Thanksgiving weekend. I took some extra days off."

"That's perfect, then. Cancel them because I'm sure the rec center could use you. You finish this time in this calendar year, or you spend ten days in the new year in jail. Your choice."

It's not fair.

"I suggest you head over there now. I'll tell Mr. Ellison you're coming. Get there before 5:00."

"What happens then?"

"You turn into a pumpkin." He laughed at his own joke.

"You're not going to tell him what I... what I did, are you?" She could feel her cheeks color.

He took pity on her as he made a point of looking at his watch. "Only what he needs to know for what they do there. Now, you better get going."

LACIE WAS SO WORRIED about leaving her new Subaru Outback in the dilapidated neighborhood she was looking back at it as she rounded the corner of the rec center building, and she never saw the blow coming. The teenager's arm caught her in her midsection hard enough to knock her down and take the wind out of her.

She sputtered for air, unable to talk or stand after she fell. She could hear a girl talking to her, but she was more interested in breathing again than in what was being said.

A face appeared right in front of hers. Words drifted into her consciousness through her haze. "We're going to help you up."

She was lifted and then she was toppling again before the

teenage boy on one side of her hauled her back into himself.

Everything after that was a blur until she was inside, had caught her breath, and found Will surrounded by nearly two dozen school aged kids.

LACIE REALIZED THE SHORT, husky, very pretty young woman Will was introducing her to was one who had been outside with the teenage boy when she heard her speak. *Was the guy her boyfriend? Maybe he wasn't as young as I thought.*

She was so taken aback by the curvy, raven-haired Sofia and by the passion the younger woman so obviously had for the center, she kept putting her foot in her mouth. *She looks like she's about sixteen. She acts like she's older than me, though, and with the weight of the world on her shoulders.*

Nothing was coming out right. As she followed Sofia outside, she vowed to herself to shut up and do whatever it took to help the center and the woman with so much obvious love for it short of letting her employers and coworkers know why she was going to be changing her working hours so she could get all her community service time in before the end of the year. *I don't need to lose my job right now, not this close to a promotion I've been working for forever. I'm on my way up. I can't screw that up.*

HEAVEN WAS SITTING at the bar drinking a thirteen-dollar margarita when Lacie finally made it to Tamayo. She cringed when she saw it. *I hope she's not assuming I'm buying tonight.*

She looped a leg over the empty stool next to her and pasted on a smile. "I hope you haven't been waiting long."

Heaven took a careful sip before looking her way. "A little bit." She indicated the drink. "That's my second. Want one?"

"Thanks, but I'll pass. Not my thing." *Me and tequila do not get along...*

"A beer then?"

"No. Actually, coffee sounds amazing."

The other woman made a pouting face. "You're not being any fun."

"It's Monday, we have to work tomorrow... I'm just not feeling it."

"You never have a drink with me when we go out. I've seen you drink."

"We've only been out two or three times." *We spend most of the time when we're together in bed, so...*

Heaven changed the subject. "So, where were you? I tried to find you around 5:00 to see if we could come over here a little early. I thought we could grab a drink and dinner and then go back to your house for a while."

Her intent was obvious to Lacie. She sidestepped both the question and the implication, saying instead, "I'm starved. Let's get a table."

"So," Heaven asked, "what are you thinking for Thanksgiving?"

With her fork poised in mid-air over her enchiladas, Lacie paused. "In what regard?"

"Um, your plans?"

The other woman's tone was grating to Lacie. She tried to ignore it. "I have nothing big planned."

"You took Wednesday through the weekend off. I saw it in the HR log."

Overstepping your boundaries as an executive assistant, I see. "I have some things it's the perfect time to get done at home before the weather gets too horrible. The company practically shuts down during that time, anyway. Why?"

"I was thinking we could get together and do something."

"It's just me. I rarely do a big meal or anything."

"That's not what I meant, but since you brought it up, you'll be alone for the holiday?"

"Yes." *Sort of... I don't know, now. Probably.*

"Oh, wow! We could go somewhere! A nice, long weekend away. Wouldn't that be amazing?"

Her excitement seemed contrived to Lacie. *I should have seen that coming. Probably her plan all along.* She turned the tables. "What do you usually do for Thanksgiving?"

Heaven pulled a face. "It's boring. I spend it with my folks and my brothers and their families. Everyone spends the entire day arguing over football - all the guys, anyway. I always feel like a fifth wheel."

So, travel was the plan. She pretended to give the idea a moment's thought, then shook her head slowly. "I just can't do it. Not this year. Sorry."

The pouting face look returned.

Don't feel bad for her. Don't feel bad. She's a big girl. She'll be fine.

It didn't take long for Heaven to regroup. "At least say you'll come to dinner with my family then; be my date. I hate the thought of you being all alone."

Ouch. Trapped. "I don't mind... and, like I said, I have things I need to do." She didn't even sound convincing to herself.

"It's just for half a day. You'll have four more days to do that stuff, and maybe even do me." Heaven winked at her.

Not subtle at all. "Half a day?"

"My family is in Fort Collins. Might be a little snowy getting up there and back in a couple weeks. So, anyway, will you come with me?"

Seeing no way out of the trap she'd walked right into, Lacie gave in. "Yes. Sure. It will be nice." *Or not. Probably not.*

3

MO' MONEY

Tuesday, November 12th
Sun Valley Community Recreation Center
Denver, Colorado

Sofia hustled toward the door juggling two grocery bags of snacks. She had to park more than a block from the center when she found a Subaru Outback parked in the spot that was usually open near the door at the time she arrived. She knew school would let out in minutes and fifteen minutes after that the center would be alive with about two dozen kids with all of their homework, hunger, and multiple other issues to deal with.

Inside, she found Lacie already there, talking with Will. She ignored the other woman and focused on the director instead. "Sorry," she said. "Britt didn't have any late classes today, so I drove myself in. I had a heck of a time finding a parking spot."

"I wasn't worried," Will said. "You never let us down. In fact, I was just telling Lacie here that you're like the Energizer Bunny."

Sofia felt a blush creep into her cheeks as she glanced the other woman's way. "I see you managed to leave work pretty early." *I didn't think we'd ever see you again.* She noted Lacie's blue jeans and her Old Navy hoodie. *Casual Tuesday? Even so, she looks good.* She glanced down at her own worn jeans and the boots she'd gotten for Christmas two years before. They were clean and serviceable, but they looked dull and dingy next to Lacie's.

Lacie waited until Sofia looked back up, and she smiled. "I rearranged my schedule."

"Great." Lacie handed the bags off to Will, who took in the contents and gave her a questioning look. She waved him off as she moved toward the rail of coat hooks on the wall and peeled off her jacket. She hung it next to Lacie's short ski jacket, which was occupying the end hook she usually used. It occurred to her the offending Subaru outside probably belonged to Lacie, too.

Trailing her, Lacie asked, "So, you did you have class today, then?"

Sofia nodded. "Sorry. We can chat later. We have to get set up for the kids."

Forty minutes later, with several children in attendance and the daily process of working on homework underway, Sofia stood and backed away from the tables for a breather. She nodded to Lacie to follow her lead. She walked into the tiny kitchenette, took out her keys and started unlocking the cabinets where Will had stashed the snacks away. She took out a packet of generic chocolate sandwich cookies, noted the cookie count, and breathed a sigh of relief that one packet would be enough for the day's group of kids.

She handed Lacie a stack of napkins and the cookies and pointed. "Lay twenty-two napkins out on that counter and put two cookies on each. I'll get the juice out." *Feels so weird telling her what to do.*

Lacie didn't move right away. "Did you buy these out of your own pocket?"

Sofia made a half shrugging motion. "We're short of funds, like I've been saying. We get a bit of extra funding in January, but we have some things we have to get through between now and then, so we're conserving the little we have right now."

"Okay, so when you have money, what do you usually give them to eat?"

"Not cookies. No sugar at all, if we can help it." She shook her head. "Sweets are usually for special occasions. These were only a couple dollars, so... " She shrugged. *Best I could do.* "Grapes or sliced apples, or carrot sticks, celery and dip go over well with most of them too, but that stuff costs a lot more, so—"

"I'll bring some veggies and fruit tomorrow."

"No, it's okay, really. You don't have to do that."

Lacie gave her a megawatt grin that made her heart flip. "I want to. I want to help. I can't promise I can do it every day, but I'll do as much as I can."

Maybe I misjudged her. "That would be nice, but please don't feel obligated."

Lacie changed the subject as she started laying napkins along the countertop. "So, you never answered my question; did you have class today?"

"Yes. I have a light schedule all the way around this semester. I, uh... went to the store right after class."

"When do you graduate?"

Sofia sighed. "Technically, I'm done at the end of this semester. I'll have my bachelor's finished a semester early."

Lacie looked over her shoulder at her. "Technically?"

"I start my Master's in the fall. Social work degrees don't get you very far unless you have your Master's, not where I want to go in the field, anyway."

"Where's that?"

Sofia knocked a cup over, spilling apple juice on the countertop. "Oh!" Some of the chilled juice dripped down onto her pants. With the jug still in hand, she jumped backwards. Juice sloshed out of the wide mouth opening, spilling over her hand and splashing her face and shirt.

Lacie grabbed up some napkins and rushed to Sofia's side where she dabbed with them at the younger women's shirt and pants.

At the touch of Lacie's hands, goosebumps formed along her arms, and she shuddered.

"Cold, huh?"

"Pardon?"

"The juice, it's cold, isn't it?"

Sofia stopped Lacie and took the napkins from her. "It's okay... not too bad. I can get it." She stifled the urge to suck in a huge gulp of air.

"You're a little wet there, Miss Sofia," Clevon said a few minutes later as the kids filed through the kitchenette to grab their snacks and came back out. "Have an accident?" He pointed at her pants, his implication clear.

"No. I did not have an accident. Did you?" She pointed at the teenager's face.

Several of the older kids jeered at him as he took his seat, saying, "I don't wanna embarrass you, so I'm gonna let that go. Besides, we have a visitor." He looked Lacie's way and nodded.

Lacie laughed. "Don't hold back on my account. And, I'm not a visitor. I'll be around for a while."

"Wait a minute!" He snapped his fingers. "I know you! You were the lady outside last night!"

"My, aren't you an observant genius, Clevon?" Sofia said, needling him. "She's been here for the past hour."

"Excuse me," Lacie called her out on her teasing. "But, aren't you supposed to be learning to be a social worker?"

Sofia knew exactly where Lacie was headed with her feigned indignation. "Yes. And he's training to be a stand-up comedian. He needs to learn how to handle hecklers." She passed along her reasoning all the while watching Clevon out of the side of her eye as he attempted to watch the reactions of Whitney, a girl his age, to the exchange.

Whitney was ignoring his antics as she helped a much younger boy reach his juice cup. She noticed another teen girl, Nelda, was giving Whitney the side eye.

Sofia shot a glance at Lacie. She wasn't looking Clevon's way anymore. *I'm going to have to keep a closer eye on him, but if he's smitten, it explains some of his horsing around and joking around.*

"I'll lock up, Will," Sofia said. "You look whipped today."

He nodded. "I've got a headache; I have to admit. I've been on the phone most of the day trying to line up donors and trying to work out something for the holiday parade. But I know you had to park a ways away. It's dark, it's cold... "

Lacie caught his drift. "I'll stay and drive her over to her car when we're done. I'm parked right outside."

He gave it a moment's thought. "I guess that would be okay. Gives you two a chance to talk a little more than you've been able to, anyway."

I'm not so sure it's a good thing. Sophia interrupted. "What's going on with the parade?"

"I've got a twenty-foot trailer promised on donation and a truck with a driver that will pull it with several of the kids on it all lined up. I just need to figure out how we're going to decorate it."

"Leave that to me," Sofia said.

"Deal." He gave in easily. "I'll push that to the side then and start puzzling over the Christmas party."

ONCE HE WAS out the door, Lacie turned to Sofia and asked, "Can you show me what to do to lock up, then can we please talk about the center, the kids, the parade, this party, and anything else that comes to mind? Spend a few minutes with me tonight, if you can?"

"A few minutes? Do you have a few hours?" Sophia cracked a smile, but it didn't extend to her voice. When the older woman just shook her head, she gave in. "Okay. But I want to know more about why you're here too." *Because there's something going on here that no one is telling me.*

"Like what?"

As she clicked the lock over on the front door to keep others from coming in, she replied, "Like are you really from the city, and here to take us over or, even worse, shut us down?"

A look of shock crossed Lacie's face. "That's what you think?"

"What else should I think?"

"No, Sofie, no."

"Sofia. No one calls me Sofie." She pushed open the ladies' room door and checked that no one was hiding out inside. She looked up at the window high on the far wall. *Closed and locked.*

"Oh, sorry," Lacie was saying from behind her. "I just... you're so young. That's kind of how I was thinking of you."

"I'm twenty-two."

"And you have the weight of the world on your shoulders. I'm here to help the center for a ... at least through the holidays and maybe even longer. I have a little money, but more than that, I have a lot of experience in planning, technology, business development, and—"

"This isn't a business." She turned away from the other woman and moved toward the men's room to repeat the same process as she'd done with the ladies' room.

"You're right, it's not. Not up front. But, on the back end, it needs to run more like one. Getting grants. Getting donations. Managing funds. Getting equipment and programming. Drawing more... clients. I think I can help with a lot of that."

Sophia took a deep breath. "That's great, but first things first. We need to figure out this parade - which will give us some visibility in Denver, outside of this neighborhood - and we need to give these kids some kind of Christmas... them and their families."

"Do *any* of them come from families with means to give them a meaningful holiday on their own?"

Sophia scoffed. "Do you really need to ask?"

"Fair point. And, for the record, you have a sassy streak in you. I thought social workers were supposed to be—"

"Pushovers? Not hardly."

"No, that's not the word I was looking—" She was interrupted by the ringing of her cell phone. She pulled it out and looked at it, then swiped ignore.

"If you need to take that... "

"No. It's okay... just a friend. I can get back to her later."

"Girlfriend?" Sofia did a mental head slap. *Why did I ask that?*

"Sort of. I mean, yes, I guess. It's early. We just started dating."

"Oh."

Lacie asked, "That doesn't bother you?"

"No, no. It's fine."

"Do you have a girlfriend?"

Sofia was stricken. She tried to keep her voice steady as she answered, "Me? No."

Lacie gave her a long look. When Sofia said nothing else, she said, "Sorry. I guess I read you wrong."

"I guess you did." She rushed past Lacie to the kitchen where she started double checking cupboard stock and switching out trash bags.

"We'll put these by the back door," she said, pointing at the bags. "Will, will take them out to the dumpster in the morning, once it's light."

Once they'd moved the trash to the back door, Lacie pointed at the tall table with barstool style chairs some of the older kids liked to use to do their homework. "Can we sit and talk for a few minutes?" When Sophia nodded, they took seats, but before they even began to chat, Lacie's cell phone buzzed with a text message.

Sophia read the name, 'Heaven' upside down, before Lacie picked up the phone from the table, silenced it and laid it face down.

"You should probably take that. It might be important."

"It's fine. Tell me about this parade, first of all."

"The Parade of Lights."

Lacie gave her a confused look.

"Don't tell me you've never been?" At the shake of the other woman's head, Sofia went on, incredulous, "How long have you lived in Denver?"

"Since college so twenty-some years. I grew up in Oklahoma. Let's just say Denver was a little more welcoming."

"And you've never been to the holiday parade?"

"Didn't realize they had one. Santa Claus and that whole deal?"

"Yes, and it's at night." Lacie shivered visibly, but her reaction didn't dampen Sofia's enthusiasm. "Everything you'd have in a daytime parade, but all lit up."

"Sounds cold." She made an exaggerated shiver to punctuate her statement.

"It's a lot of fun, so you don't even think about it. The center tries to do a float every year. It didn't look good for this year, but Will came through with a truck and trailer, so I'm going to do everything I can to pull it off. The kids love it."

"So a float?"

Sofia nodded. "One as many of the kids who can come will have room to ride on even with all the decorations."

"So, what's the plan to decorate it?"

"Lights. Lots of lights. This parade is more about the lights than the actual design of the float."

"I see. And this brings 'visibility' to the center?" She made air quotes.

"In the coolest possible way."

Lacie grinned, her head shaking. "You sound like one of the kids here."

She tensed as she said, "I'm not."

"Oh, believe me, I know it. No offense, I just like your enthusiasm." She asked, "So, do we have lights?"

Sofia let out a huff of breath. "That's the thing. The parade is always early in December. We dismantle the float after that and give the lights to the kids and around in the community. We start from scratch every year."

"Oh. Okay."

Sofia tensed again at the implication in her tone. "I get that it's not a way to 'run a business,' like you've talked about," she mimicked Lacie's air quotes, "but it's a little bit of goodwill we can do for this community that brings a lot of joy."

"I'm sorry. I didn't mean to give you the wrong impression. I get it... I do."

Sofia sat back; her arms folded across her chest. "I don't think you do. Our purpose here is to serve this community. Give people a hand up. Some of these kids will never leave here; this little piece of Denver will be all they ever know, but some of them will. Some of them will make it out. We do everything in our power to help them while they're still willing to come to us, give them some hope."

Lacie picked up on the point within her point. "They don't keep doing after-school programs once they're in high school, do they?"

"Not here, they don't. We don't have the staff for that. A lot of them don't even stick with us through middle school, anyway. Our time to get through to them is pretty limited."

THE RIDE to Sofia's car from the center was a quiet one. It was dark and cold out, the streets deserted, even though it was just after 6:00 PM. Sofia knew it wouldn't stay that way. *The dealers will all be working their usual corners, and the junkies and addicts will be out looking for another fix.*

Lacie pulled over where Sofia told her to and turned to her. "I'm sorry. Really. I grew up hard. I'll tell you about it some time, but my point is, I can relate because I made it out myself and I can help... if you'll let me." When Sofia didn't respond, she continued, "I don't pretend to know anything about social work or about kids. Obviously I don't have a lot of knowledge about the city I've called home for years, but I know about making do, finding a way, raising funding, and a whole host of other things. I think we'd make a good team, if you'll have me."

Sofia gave her a long look. The Outback was dark, illuminated only by the dashboard lights, but she thought she could see a gleam in Lacie's eyes. Her heart leaped, but she mentally steadied herself. "This is very different for you, isn't it?"

"You have no idea."

She gave it several long seconds of thought. "Well, it will be a challenge for you, then. See you tomorrow?"

"Absolutely."

Sofia gave her a nod and got out of the car.

4

C-SUITE

Wednesday, November 13th
Tech Success, Inc.
Denver, Colorado

L acie rocked backward in her chair, hands on top of her head, and stared at her computer screen, but she really didn't see it. Her thoughts were on Sofia. *Such a passionate firebrand about the center and the kids, but so insecure personally. An adorable ball of contradictions...* She sighed. *She's just so young.*

She mentally kicked herself. *Focus. No relationships. That won't to get you to the C-suite.*

Heaven rounded the corner and walked right into Lacie's cubicle, drawing her out of her reverie. "Oh, so you are here!"

"Pardon? I've been here all morning."

"You left really early yesterday, and I didn't see you getting your coffee this morning."

Stalking much? She pointed to her ceramic mug.

"Oh. Don't you usually go to Crave for coffee?"

"Sometimes." *Only on payday as a little treat to myself.* "They aren't open until 7:00. I was in before that." *A couple hours before that.* She realized her error too late.

"In early, leaving early? What gives?"

She gave Heaven a half shrug. "I've got a lot of work to do."

Heaven scratched her head. "That doesn't make any sense. Why would you leave early, then?"

"I'm working on a special project in the afternoons, but I still need to get my regular work done." *And then some. That VP slot and the cushy office that goes with it aren't guaranteed to be mine.*

"For the company?"

"Hmm?"

"Your special project? It's for the company? I haven't heard about any special project."

"IT department thing," Lacie lied. She tried to feel a little remorse for her untruth, but it wasn't there.

Heaven wrinkled her nose in distaste. "You can have all that computer stuff. If I didn't have to use one, I wouldn't."

Shocker. "You do work for a tech company, you know."

Heaven glossed over that, instead saying, "Anyway, since you've been ignoring me the past couple of days, how would you like to take me to lunch?"

"Oh, sorry. Can't," Lacie answered quickly. Then, registering what Heaven said, "And I haven't been ignoring you. It's only Wednesday morning. We had dinner Monday night."

Hand on her hip, the bottle blond wasn't having it. "And I treated."

Her implication clear, Lacie tried to compromise. "I've been coming in early and working through lunch so I can leave early and focus on my... on the project. How about this? How about I take you out this Saturday? We can spend the evening together."

"Mmm," Heaven said with a finger to her lips. She tapped

them a couple times and then responded, "No, not Saturday. How about Friday? There's a group playing at Dazzle on Friday night that I'd like to hear."

Not my kind of music. "I'm not sure what time I'm going to be able to break away on Friday."

"They don't take the stage until ten-ish. They're the headliners."

"I'll think about it, but no promises." *Not negotiating. It's a hard no on that.* "Look around though, and see what you might like to do on Saturday instead. Now, I'm sorry, but I really need to get back to work."

KENDALL STOPPED in the cubicle entryway when Heaven left. "How's it going?"

Her tone told Lacie she'd heard everything and knew how things were. She sighed and waved her friend in.

"I take it you haven't told her anything?"

"No, and I'm not going to. She can't keep her mouth shut and I can't risk her blabbing up the chain and messing up my chance at VP of Tech."

Kendall waved a hand as she took a seat in Lacie's only side chair. "You have that in the bag."

"What? Do you know something?"

Her friend chuckled. "No, but relax. You're a shoe in. You run rings around all the other business analysts."

Lacie leaned in and whispered back, "Who are all straight, mostly white, and males." *Damn cubicle life. I hope she's right. I need a proper office.*

"One day, you'll be the CTO of this company."

That's the goal. "Let's not get ahead of ourselves."

"Still, I hope she doesn't find out. She can be an ass about stuff."

Snapping back to reality, Lacie agreed. "Me too."

"So, how's your *project* going?"

"It's different. Hildalgo sent me to a rec center over near the stadium."

"Seriously? There are some sketchy neighborhoods over there."

"This one isn't too bad, just a little run down. So is the center, for that matter. They need a lot of help. I'm not sure what his association with it is, but I can see why he sent someone... me... there."

"Anything I can do to help?"

Lacie leaned back, but kept her voice low. "No. Not yet, at least. There are some things coming up that Sofia - that's my... boss over there, I guess that's what you'd call her - that are going to take some work. I'll let you know."

"Sofia?"

"What?"

"You smiled when you said her name."

"She's the social worker... almost social worker there. She hasn't graduated from college yet and she's around half my age. She's twenty-two."

"But she's gay?"

Lacie rolled her eyes. "Yes. At least, I'm pretty sure she is anyway, and apparently way in the closet."

"Is she cute?"

Lacie hesitated too long.

"You like her!"

"Shh!" A blush crept up Lacie's neck to her cheeks.

"Yes, she's cute. Latina, I think. There's a hint of a Spanish accent there, but no, I'm not going there. A, she's young. Way too young. B, she's in the closet, and C, you know work comes first and last for me. I don't do committed relationships."

"Interesting."

Lacie groaned. "What is?"

"You don't do committed relationships, but clearly you're thinking of her like that."

She ignored that, saying instead, "There's one more problem, too. Even if I wanted to have any sort of chance with her, I can't. She hasn't been told why I'm helping there, and I can't tell her."

"Why not? She's a social worker or nearly so, right?"

"Nearly."

"Then I'm sure she'd understand. She's probably heard it all before."

"Not this! And I'm sure I'd die of embarrassment if she found out."

'NOTHING IS CLOSE TO THERE,' Lacie muttered to herself as she hustled into Trader Joe's a few miles and a fifteen-to-twenty-minute drive in traffic from the rec center.

Knowing she had only ten minutes to spare, she hit the produce section and grabbed apples and grapes, baby carrots, and celery. She gave some thought to having the kids help her julienne full sized, organic carrots, but she wasn't sure if the rec center had any knives. *Probably not.* She put the celery stalks back and picked up a container of cut pieces instead.

There were several choices for veggie and fruit dips, but she went for basic choices rather than exotic ones except for a chipotle style dip which she was sure at least some of the kids would like. She grabbed a couple of tubs of fresh salsa and guacamole too, knowing blue and white corn tortillas were normally stationed close to the checkout.

She wasn't wrong. She picked up two bags of each and got in line. *This is going to set me back at least fifty bucks. But, then again, I would have spent that taking Heaven to lunch.*

As she checked out and toted her purchases to her car, she

had Sofia rather than Heaven on her mind. *What if I told her? What would she think of me?* She mentally kicked herself. *Kendall is right. I've got it bad for her, and I just don't need that right now. I need to focus.*

Her mind flashed back to the summer and her fortieth birthday as she drove. She hadn't been planning to celebrate. Kendall had other ideas. She convinced her to go out with her, her wife, and some of their friends, have a good time and not think about work for once. *I didn't know any of them, thank God. What a nightmare that night turned into.*

It had all started innocently enough on a Friday night. They'd met at a lesbian bar and had a few drinks. The place got crowded, the air conditioning not keeping up. Someone had suggested they take their party to 'the lake.' Drunk on tequila shots, she'd agreed. Someone else drove. She wasn't aware then that it would be a couple days before she'd see her little Subaru again.

At the lake - she couldn't even remember which one - she'd switched to beer because that was all the convenience store they'd stopped at on the way carried.

She couldn't remember who suggested skinny dipping. She did remember hesitating at first, but joined in when everyone started stripping off their work outfits in the heat and humidity and jumping into the cool water.

When the cops showed up, more than half their crew was out and dressed. Embarrassed, she had refused to get out of the water. An officer tried to snag her from the sandy beachhead, but he failed and toppled in. She laughed as she fell on him. She was unceremoniously hauled up by a couple of other officers and cuffed then pushed into a sitting position, naked on the sand.

Her friends pleaded for her release, but the officers weren't swayed. They all got warnings for their indecent exposure. She was hauled off to the county lock-up for indecent exposure, resisting arrest, and for assault on a police officer.

Waking up in a holding cell a few hours later, my stomach churning was the low point of my life... until my arraignment Saturday afternoon. I can't tell Sofia any of this. Hell, I can't even look Will straight in the face. How am I going to work with this?

AS SHE STARTED down Decatur Street, she spotted Sofia walking away from a bus stop a city bus was pulling away from. She cruised alongside, pulled to a stop, and put the window down. "That's a cold walk. Hop in!"

The younger woman didn't hesitate. "Thanks. It's not that far, but the wind is really kicking up today."

"I take it your friend has class today? It is Wednesday, after all."

"Brittany, yes. She'll pick me up at 5:30."

"Convenient."

"It worked out this semester. Saves me on gas and lets me do a little more for the kids."

Lacie jerked a thumb toward her back seat. "I've got your back today and tomorrow."

Sofia looked in the backseat. "Wow. I... I don't know what to say. Thanks!"

"No thanks necessary," she said, as she stopped and began maneuvers to parallel park in the empty spot in front of the center. "We better get a move on. We'll have hungry kids showing up soon."

5

KID PROBLEMS

Sofia marveled as she looked in the bags. "Chips and salsa? The kids are going to love you."

"The salsa is fresh and there's fresh guacamole too. I mean, I'm not sure how many of them will eat that, but I like it."

"Will likes it," Sofia said. "He'll be happy to help you eat it."

Lacie shot the younger woman a look. "Not your thing, I take it?"

She shook her head no. "Never cared for it. The only way I'll eat it is in my mother's locro."

"Um, you lost me there. Locro?"

"It's a potato soup with cheese and avocado. She makes it a lot this time of year if she can get avocados."

"Never heard of it, but it sounds good."

"I'll bring some in for you."

Lacie smiled. "That sounds nice, but don't go out of your way to—"

Sofia waved her off. "It's no big deal. I bring it in for Will, too. In fact, he's been down to the ranch and eaten half a pan of it."

"You have a ranch?" *With horses?*

"No. I live on one with my mother and father." She sighed.

"It's not theirs either. I wish it was, but that's just not going to happen to them anytime soon. My dad manages the horse stables and I help out when I can. We have a small home on the property near the ranch manager's place."

Lacie was about to say something else when the sounds of children's voices entering the center filtered into the kitchenette, stopping her mid-question. The two women made quick work of putting everything away temporarily and went out to tend to the kids.

LACIE PULLED Sofia aside a half hour later. "DeMarco, is that his name?" She tipped her head toward the ten-year-old sitting at the end of a table, staring off into space.

Sofia nodded. "What about him?"

"He won't do his homework. Says he'll be out of school by the end of the week."

"He probably will be."

"What? Why? What do you know?"

"It's not specific to him, Lacie," she said, adopting an even tone. "These kids, their families, they're transient, especially if they're not in public housing, but then even some of them move around a lot, too. Their caregivers, whomever they may be, skip rent for a month or two then either get evicted or move on before the next payment is due. Look around the room at all the kids faces. At least a couple of them, probably more, won't be here by Thanksgiving."

Lacie looked surprised. "That's awful."

"The facts of life. The last couple of months of the year are always the hardest on the poor and underemployed."

"You're too young to be so world-weary."

"You keep calling me young. I've been working with these

kids for eight or nine years now. I started coming in here with my father when I was a teenager."

"He's a social worker?"

"No. I told you, he's a rancher. He manages horses. But people did for him growing up and for me. He wanted to make sure I always give back by doing for others."

Lacie backtracked, "Speaking of Thanksgiving, what happens here?"

"We're closed that day. A big church up the street puts on an annual Thanksgiving Day feast that usually features two or three of the current Denver Broncos... guaranteed to draw a crowd and make sure everyone that wants one gets a decent meal." *And my family and I usually pitch in and help serve.*

SOFIA TRIED to listen without appearing to be listening as Lacie talked with Clevon. A pang of jealousy hit her as she watched their easy banter. She had a soft spot for the teenager. He was the only kid present who'd been coming to the center for as long as she had, and longer. She remembered waiting outside for him as he walked down the street from the school after his first day of kindergarten. He chattered non-stop, giving her the blow by blow of his day. He was the class clown, even back then.

"Is there something, if it didn't cost a lot," Lacie was asking him, "that you'd want for Christmas?"

He was quick to answer, "An iPhone of my own or one of the new Galaxy phones. Grandma can't afford that."

She backhanded him lightly on the shoulder. "I said that didn't cost the earth and the stars."

He rubbed his chin like a thoughtful adult would do and eyeballed her. "Why?"

"Just curious. Christmas is coming. I hear they have a party here. You ever been to one of them?"

"Yeah. I been."

"Fun?"

"For the little kids, I guess."

"Not for you?"

"It's okay. Some of it is fun."

"What parts are fun for you?"

"Well, there's always lots of food."

Lacie laughed. "And you're a bottomless pit."

He smacked his hands against his chest. "Takes a lot to look this good!"

Whitney walked by, shaking her head.

"It does," he called after her. He watched her walk away.

Lacie caught Sofia's eye and tipped her head just slightly toward Whitney.

Good, Sophia thought. *Another set of eyes on them now.* She moved a little closer to the two of them.

Lacie picked up where she left off. "What else was fun about the parties?"

Clevon glanced at Sophia before saying, "It's more fun when she sets them up than Will. Sometimes she lets us put on a show for whoever will come and watch. At least, she did when I was back in elementary school."

"Hmm. Bet we could arrange that this year too," Lacie said. "So, can we put you down for a dance number?"

"What? No! I mean, I dance, but I ain't dancing for no audience or nothing."

Sophia cringed at his grammar but chose to pick her battles. Lacie was getting him to open up about something she and Will were worried about, and the intel was good.

"Christmas carol solo, then?"

"No! I ain't singing. That's for the little kids."

"What then?"

Her light-hearted tone with him told Sofia she already knew what the answer was.

"If we're really doing this, I want to do some stand-up. A little routine."

Sofia jumped in then. "IF we do this, big IF, we might consider that, but you have to keep it clean. No swearing. Nothing crude."

Clevon nodded vigorously. "Okay. Okay. I can do that... I can do that."

"No yo mama jokes, or yo sister jokes, either."

"Ouch. Man, that's half my stuff!"

"It's a Christmas show."

"Now, hang on," Lacie suggested, "If you cleaned them up... made them holiday themed, even. Don't say 'so fat,' or 'so ugly,' for example. Say stuff like, Santa's suit is so red, he was mistaken for a matador."

Clevon raised an eyebrow. "That's terrible. Not funny at all."

"Yeah," Lacie said, "I know, but you get the idea. I'm sure you can do better."

He gave it some thought, then conceded, "That might work. It would be different."

Sophia gave him a boost. "If anyone can do it, you can."

"But how long would I have?"

Sofia looked at Lacie and spread her hands.

Lacie asked, "Taking out all of that, how much material do you think you can come up with between now and the party, which is... I don't even know when it is."

"Christmas Eve," Sophia supplied.

She watched for Lacie's reaction, but Clevon answered, "I can probably do about five minutes, or so."

"Okay," Lacie said, "we'll assign you three minutes because you might be nervous and talk fast and maybe, if you're good, we won't hook you if you go a little over your time."

He laughed. "Hook me, ha ha. That reminds me though... "

"Of what?" They both asked.

"What I want for Christmas that doesn't cost much. I've always wanted to go fishing. When my grandpop was alive, he used to go. I always wanted to go with him, but Grandma said I was too little, I'd fall in, and neither one of us could swim."

"Do you have snow boots?" Lacie asked him.

"He—, I mean heck no. I wouldn't wear no snow boots."

"You're going to need them if you want to go fishing this time of year," Sophia said.

WHILE SOPHIA WAS WATCHING Nelda hustle to catch up with Clevon, Brittney's old truck rattled to a stop in the street alongside Lacie's Outback. Despite the cold, she leaned over, rolled down the window and called out to Will before he rounded the corner with the young charges he was walking toward home, "Hey, Will, buddy! How's it going?"

Will waved back. "Good to see you Britt."

"Before you even have to ask, I already told Sofia I'd help over the holidays with the parade and stuff."

He gave her a grin and a thumbs up before moving on.

Sophia laughed from her position on the sidewalk in front of the door and told her, "You made his night." She turned to Lacie. "You can head out if you want. I'll wait for Will to get back before I leave. He's only usually a few minutes."

A car rumbled toward them, prompting Sofia to glance over and tell Brittney, "You better park for a few minutes. There's actually a space, even." She pointed up the block a little distance.

As Sofia and Lacie looked on, Britt started to pull away. The old truck stalled out. She attempted to restart it, but nothing happened. Brittany opened her door, jumped down and waved at the other driver to squeeze around her before she headed toward them. "I'm just going to give it a minute. I don't want to flood it."

"It's so far out of your way, we really appreciate this," Sofia said to Lacie from the passenger seat of her Outback.

"How do you know it's out of my way?"

Brittany spoke up from the back seat, "Highlands Ranch isn't on anyone's way."

Lacie reassured them, "I live in Greenwood Village. You're, what, nine or ten miles further south? And, it's not like I'm doing anything tonight."

"No date?" Brittany asked.

Sofia turned her head and shot her friend a look.

Lacie took the question in stride. "Nope. No date."

"But you have a girlfriend, right?"

Sophia was mortified at her prying and called out, "Brittany!"

"What? I can't get to know our new friend and rescuer?"

Sophia caught Lacie's grin out of the corner of her eye.

"So, you two have already talked about me."

She coughed, nearly choking at Lacie's matter-of-fact response. Lacie reached over and thumped her back between her shoulder blades without taking her eyes off the road.

"Sorry," Sophia sputtered. "She asked who you were the other night, and... well, that's a lie," she admitted. "I mean, she asked Monday night, but you told me about your girlfriend last night and—"

Lacie put her out of her misery. "She's not really my girlfriend. We've been out on a few dates. I'm pretty focused on my career at this stage of my life."

Brittany ignored that and dived right back in. "Have you slept with her?"

"Oh. My. God, Brittany! Let it go already!" She could feel the burn in her cheeks.

Lacie had the good grace not to answer. "Who am I dropping off first?" she asked, instead.

Britt said, "You can just drop us both at Sophia's. I texted my fiancé. He's going to pick me up there when he gets off work and we'll ride back in to work on my truck."

"Okay. So, how about we talk about something that won't trigger coughing spasms in Sofia here? Tell me about this Christmas party."

Thank heaven! Sofia launched right in. "We have it every year. I mean, the center does. It's always on Christmas Eve."

"Why is that?"

"That makes it feel more like Christmas for everyone. We invite all the kids' families, but we've always tried not to turn anyone in the neighborhood away."

"That's a lot of people who could potentially show up," Lacie said.

"True, but it's never been a problem."

Brittany added, "There's usually enough food for an Army and Santa always has gifts put back for any kids that show up that don't use the center for the after-school program."

Lacie glanced over her shoulder at Britt. "How long have you been involved in the party?"

"As long as Sofia and her dad."

"She's being modest," Sophia said. "She's worked for the center on and off over the last several years too and volunteered at times in between."

"What's different about this year, besides the lack of funding?"

Sophia let out a small sigh while Brittany piped up, "That's pretty much it. There was always a lot of food. Entertainment—"

"Well, that was usually done by the kids," Sofia said.

Brittany went on, "True. And each kid gets a semi-big gift, and then there were small gift bags for the adults with... small things in them and, if there's enough money, some smaller gifts for the kids too... depending on how much money there was."

As LACIE WORKED her way back a long drive to the home Sophia and her parents occupied, Sofia volunteered, "Come in and meet my mother and dad. And, mom will probably want to feed you for being our rescuer tonight."

"I'll meet them, but I couldn't impose for dinner."

Brittany leaned up between the seats, "Trust me, you'll want to stay. Eva's cooking is the best. And tonight she promised some llapingachos with dinner, if I remember right."

"La, la what?"

Sophia laughed. "Llapingachos. It's a traditional potato cake dish from Ecuador, where my family is from."

"Ah. I wondered where you were from. Your coloring tells me you're not of European descent, but I didn't want to be rude."

Sophia smiled. "It's okay. I was born here, well, in the US, in New York City. We moved from there before I turned two though, so I don't really remember it."

"I'm just going to go ahead and ask, because I've always been called out for being forward anyway," Britt began from just over Lacie's shoulder, "Where are you from, yourself?"

"I was born in Oklahoma. My mother was half Cherokee, half white. My father was white."

Sofia caught the 'was' in Lacie's response by Britt focused elsewhere.

"Cherokee. That's so cool," Britt said.

Lacie shrugged it off as she stopped the car in front of the Vaca's little home. "I wasn't raised on tribal lands or with my any of my tribal heritage. My mother was, but she left the tribe to marry my father when she was seventeen."

We have more in common than I thought, Sophia thought. "Come inside," she said. "Please. My dad loves to meet the volunteers at the center."

6

OVER 40... MEET THE PARENTS

Hector Vaca was all smiles with Lacie. Lacie found him charming, and she was glad she stayed.

Sofia's mother, Eva, was cordial and served up a feast, but she seemed much more reserved to Lacie, even with her daughter. She spoke Spanish to Hector but switched to English for general conversation. It was obvious to Lacie that Sofia had more of a connection with her father than with her mother. *A true daddy's girl.*

Brittney had been right. The llapingachos were divine, all potato-y, cheesy goodness. And the conversation wasn't bad either. She could have listened to Hector and Sophia banter all night. *They have a connection I wish I had, had with my dad.*

Hector raised his water glass. "To new friends."

Lacie picked hers up half a step ahead of the other women. "Likewise. It's been a pleasure meeting all of you."

The man at the head of the table, whom she estimated was only a handful of years older than she, grinned. "You can visit any time, but you'll surely have to come back in the Spring, let me or Sophia show you around. It's not our place, but it's the place we love most in the world; isn't that right?" he asked as he looked his daughter's way.

Mid-bite, Sophia was taken by surprise. She swallowed without really chewing and began to cough.

Brittney slapped her on the back. "Are you all right?"

"Yes," she got out as she coughed into her balled fist. She was rescued from further comment when Brittney's cell phone rang loudly from the basket on the sideboard where Eva had made all of them leave their phones during dinner.

Eva gave both of the younger women a stern look. Britt ignored it as she jumped up, saying, "That's Frank's ring tone. He probably just got off work." She grabbed her phone and left the small dining alcove.

"Your house is so cute and cozy," Lacie said to Eva. "I love it."

"Thank you," was the only reply. Eva got up and began clearing plates.

Lacie stood too. "Let me help you."

The other woman, only slightly older than herself in Lacie's judgment, gave her the same frowning glare she'd given Brittney and Sophia moments before and waved her back down.

Hector, who stood when Lacie did, said, "If you'll excuse me. I need to tend to one of the mares. She's been ill."

"Do you need help, dad?"

"I'll take care of it. You have a guest."

"I hate to eat and run," Lacie said, "but you two have things you need to tend to, and I should be going. Thank you so much for dinner."

Hector gave her a small nod. "Anytime. Thank you for looking after my Sofia."

"Thank you so much for dinner, Eva," Lacie called to the woman only twenty feet away in the open kitchen.

Eva raised a hand in a goodbye gesture, but otherwise remained focused on the pot she was scrubbing in the sink.

. . .

BRITTNEY WAS on the front porch when Lacie walked outside. The younger woman had her coat on, but she was rubbing her arms against the cold.

Seeing she wasn't on the phone, Lacie said, "It's warm inside."

"Frank's only about five minutes away. When I saw Hector and Sofia head toward the stables in the Ranger, I figured I'd just wait out here. Those two, with horses... they won't be back very soon."

"Does Sofia help him a lot?"

"Him, and the ranch manager, the owner. Anytime it has to do with the horses. She's actually on the payroll as a ranch hand. So am I." She waved a hand. "She's always worked with horses; at least since I've known her. Gives trail rides, trains riders. It's her dream to take her degree, once she gets her masters, and use it in combination with an equine therapy program."

"Wow. That's great. I really had no idea, but then, I don't know her all that well. She told me about needing to go on for her masters to get very far in social work, but she never said anything about her ultimate dream."

Britt studied her for a few seconds. "Honestly? I'm surprised you got that much out of her. She's not one for opening up until you've known her a while."

I may as well ask... "Not to change the subject, but if you don't mind me asking - you don't have to answer—"

"Oh, dish! What's up?"

Lacie chuckled. "Nothing's 'up.' I was just wondering about Eva. She seems—"

"Mean?"

"No. I wouldn't say that." She shook her head. "No, I was

thinking more like reserved. And, honestly, it doesn't seem like she and Sofia get along well."

"Well enough, I suppose," Brittney said. "They don't fight, I mean, but they aren't close at all. Never really have been, but they really grew apart during Sofia's freshman year."

"Baby leaving the nest sort of thing?"

"Not that, so much." Britt leaned in and looked over her shoulder at the front door, which Lacie had made sure to pull closed behind her. "I don't know what all she might have told you, but it's obvious to me she sees you as a kindred soul... so to speak, so between me and you, I'll tell you that Sofia figured out she preferred women over men freshman year when all freshmen had to live on campus. She fell hard for her roommate."

Ah. "Her mother didn't approve?"

"I don't know that she exactly *knew*, for sure, but Sofia is scared to death of displeasing her. Eva's very traditional in her ways. She only speaks Spanish here at home unless they have guests, and I don't count there. Never misses Mass or any of the holy days. Dotes on Sofia's older sister Concetta and her grand-children. Anyway, to save money, her parents made her move back home after our first year. It was harder for her to maintain a relationship on the down low then."

Wow. "So, she's never dated another woman since?"

"She hasn't dated anyone at all. She knows she can never measure up to Concetta in her mother's eyes, but she doesn't want to displease her even more. Her family is everything to her. Honestly, she hasn't even shown any interest in anyone at all. At least, not until you came along."

Before Lacie could respond, a pickup truck that was only a few years newer than Brittney's pulled into the driveway. "There's Frank," Brittney said. "Nice talking to you tonight. Thanks for your help."

"Anytime," Lacie said, as she followed the younger woman off the porch and made her way to her own car.

SHE'S TOO YOUNG. *She's too young. She has her whole life ahead of her.* Lacie almost missed her exit because she was so wrapped up in thinking about Sofia and about what Brittney said.

As she took the off ramp, she shifted uncomfortably in her seat. She could feel the heat in her core. It wasn't an unpleasant feeling, or even unwelcome, but she knew she couldn't act on her desire. Not with Sofia. *Not now. Not ever. Let her come to terms with her truth on her own.*

HEAVEN WAS SITTING in her car in front of her condo when she drove up.

What's she doing here? She let out a breath in a huff and drove on into her garage. She put on a smile she didn't feel while she waited for Heaven to come into the garage.

She had her oversize designer purse slung over one shoulder, but it didn't seem to balance out the bag with a restaurant logo she toted in her opposite hand as she teetered on the three-inch heels of thigh-high boots meant more for style than function.

I used to think she was sexy in a getup like that. Sofia in her worn jeans and boots flashed through her mind. Her smile broadened, but then Heaven spoke, breaking her out of her reverie.

"I've been waiting for you for it feels like forever."

"I told you I wasn't on a set schedule with this... project."

"But it's after 7:00. I just thought... Well, I don't know what I thought. I brought you dinner. It's cold now but we should be able to heat it up."

We. Of course she'd expect to share it. She held back a sigh. "I'm sorry. I've eaten. We ate in." *It's not really a lie.*

"Great. Just great." Heaven swung the restaurant bag toward her. "Can we go in, please? It's cold out here."

"I'm sorry, Heaven. I am. I didn't know you were coming tonight. I told you I'd be working late. I have to be in the office early again in the morning and all I want to do is go in, get into some sweats, and go to bed."

"Are you dumping me?"

We aren't technically a couple. "No. It's just... I'm just exhausted, and this is the way it's going to be for a while. I tried to explain that this morning." *Which seems like eons ago.*

"What about Thanksgiving?"

"What about it?"

"Are we still on for that?"

"I hope so. Probably." She wasn't so sure, but she didn't want to fight anymore.

"But you can't commit to it?"

Here we go. "No. I can't say for sure. I want to, but it depends on how things go—"

"With the project, I know. Just what is this project, again? You weren't very clear on that."

"Heaven, please, I'm really tired. I'll explain it all at work tomorrow, I promise."

"Whatever, Lacie!" She flung the bag of takeout toward her. "You may as well take it. You can eat it tomorrow while you work through lunch!"

7

FLOATING IDEAS

Thursday, November 14th
Tivoli Student Union
Denver, Colorado

Brittney set her tray down, took a bottle of flavored water off of it, and passed it to Sofia. "I got you this."

Sophia flashed her thermos. "You didn't have to do that. I have soup." She took a bite of the sandwich she'd brought from home.

"I hope you can find a job after the holidays."

"I have a job."

"You know what I mean, a paying job."

"I earn money at the ranch, same as you." She sighed internally. "But, you're right, the job fair wasn't very promising last week. I knew it was going to be tough with just a BS, but it s looking like I'm going to have to start somewhere as just a paid intern."

"The job you already have, unpaid." Britt shook her head.

"Heard anything at all from any of the equine programs?" Sophia shook her head, her sad expression telling Brittney all she needed to know.

"Have you thought about the Child Welfare departments, at least to get your foot in the door with kids somewhere?"

"Oh, yeah," Sophia said, nodding this time. "But the state has all the county run ones under a hiring freeze until next year."

"I feel so bad. I barely had to try."

Sophia knew what she meant. Britt had gotten a manager trainee position lined up months before her own graduation with a business degree. She was graduating half a year later than Sophia, on the normal university schedule.

"Can I ask you something?" Britt said, drawing her friend out of her head. When she nodded, Britt said, "About Lacie?"

Sophia became defensive. "What about her?"

"Do you think she'd help me? Give me some pointers, introduce me to some people?"

Her defensiveness turned to puzzlement. "Why would you want *her* to do those things for you?"

"Isn't she a business analyst? That's what I thought she said."

"Yes. Some company over there in the tech park."

"Exactly."

"Exactly, what? You have a job lined up, so I don't get it."

"As an underling manager at a big box store. I love retail, don't get me wrong, but Frank and I have been talking and he's made some good points. I'm going to get moved store to store as I rise through the ranks. I'm going to get all kinds of crazy hours up front and all the weekends and holidays. We were... we were hoping to settle down right after the wedding and even start a family."

Sophia grinned. "That's the first time I've heard you talk about specific plans after your wedding."

"I've talked about having kids before."

"But not specifically with Frank."

"Who else would I have them with?" They both laughed.

Sobering, Sophia said, "You don't have afternoon classes today, but you could stick around and come to the center with me. She'll be there. You two could talk. Who knows? She may help. She probably will. I don't know her all that well to say. She's volunteering there, so she's got a helping heart... though, at first, it seemed like she was a lot more business minded than child centered."

"Maybe I'll do that."

"I'd like that, and if you don't mind, I could sure use another pair of hands. We've got to figure out the Parade of Lights float."

"How's that coming?"

"It's not. Will just got a truck and trailer donated. We have to come up with some sort of design and then get the lights to cover it."

"Design shouldn't be hard. Some sort of framework. What's the theme?"

Sophia shook her head. "No clue, but I suppose Will knows. We can ask him later." She put the remains of her sandwich down and half threw up her hands. "The problem is the lights. No matter what we decide to do, we're going to need a lot and we have none... and no money."

"Donations?"

"I mean, we can try, but it's three weeks to the parade and—"

"So, we get started today. We'll sit down and make a list with Will of people who usually donate, and we'll start hitting them up right now. I'll help. It's possible Lacie will too. Maybe she knows people that will help us or she might get her company to donate."

~

Sofia and Britt were talking to Will about the float when Lacie made it in. "I have the wood," he was saying, "that we'll need to do the base construction. All the leftover materials from our spring project helping to build those raised planters for the community gardens were donated to us."

"What's the theme, Will?" Brittney chimed in.

"Something that won't resonate with most of these kids, 'Home for the Holidays'." He spread his hands. "It is what it is."

"Ouch," Sofia said. She thought for a minute and then offered, "None of these kids... right now, are technically homeless. My dad always says, 'home is where you hang your hat.' We should work from that idea with them to come up with something. That, or we disregard the theme and go a different route."

Lacie jumped in. "No. Don't second guess yourself. I think you have something there. Let's brainstorm with the kids today about what makes a home and see if we can't come up with an idea that incorporates what they think."

There were nods all around. "Good idea," Will said.

"And it's a lighted thing, Sophia tells me." She paused when she saw their surprised looks. "I've been sheltered with no kids around me for the last twenty years, okay? Anyway," she picked up where she left off, "I was talking to one of our IT guys today that does a lot of the programming for internal needs for my company... for where I work, and he said if we can come up with something we can program to music, he can help with that. He can get the equipment we need and do the programming."

Sofia's eyes grew wide. "Program our lights to music? The kids would love that. " Then, her face fell, "But the lights are the real problem."

She addressed Will. "Britt and I were talking about it earlier today. We're behind the clock for sure. We were wondering if you could give us a list of our donors we could call? We'd ask them only for lights or for money to buy lights. And, we'd need to get started right away... today."

Brittney added, "If there are any corporate donors we could tap, we'd like to start with those. We might get what we need with just one or two donations, depending on what Sophia here and the kids come up with today."

"You've done this parade in the past, right?" Lacie asked. When the other three nodded, she went on, "So how much have you typically spent?"

"Will shrugged. It's been with all the materials and the lights, a thousand dollars or so of our budget for November or December."

"That's not a lot," Lacie said. "Better than I thought."

Sophia let her annoyance show, "It's a lot when you have none of it."

Brittney put a hand on Sophia's arm. "It's okay. We'll figure it out."

"Sorry," Lacie said. "I just meant that a single corporate donor might take that on, not that the amount of money was insignificant." When no one said anything, she addressed Sophia specifically, "Why don't you leave that part to me?"

Brittany was the one to answer. "You think the company you work for would take care of everything?"

Lacie shrugged. "Uh, maybe. Regardless, though, I'll figure it out. I'm connected to some people who could help."

Sophia had Brittney help her set the two long tables the younger kids sat at to do their homework and eat their snacks, end to end. They had all the kids gather around.

She noted that Clevon sat on the far end and was surprised to see Whitney take up a position right across the table from him. It didn't surprise her to see Nelda muscle a younger kid over so she could sit on Clevon's right. *I'll have to deal with that whole situation soon.* "Okay, everybody, listen up. We have a project."

Several of the smaller children clapped their hands together. The older ones looked on with interest.

"The Parade of Lights is Friday night, December 6th. That's about three weeks away. Some of you may remember that last year we did a small float for the parade."

"Yeah," Clevon said, "We pulled it down the street in DeMarco's little red wagon."

Several of the children laughed.

"It wasn't that small," Brittney said. She glanced at DeMarco and then gave Clevon a withering look.

Sophia waved a hand at Clevon. "It wasn't, but this one is going to be bigger. Lots bigger. Will got us a flatbed trailer and a truck to pull it this year."

"Yes!" Clevon called out as he pumped a fist in the air.

"A bed?" Maya asked.

"Not like you're thinking, sweetie. It's a flat surface - kind of like a table - on wheels that a truck can pull. We can build something for the parade on top of it, and we can ride on it."

"Oh." Her response was matter of fact, but her smile spoke volumes to Sophia.

"So, we need to brainstorm some ideas for what to put on our float," Sophia said.

The kids started calling out things. "My dog," said one.

Another called out, "No, a petting zoo. People at the parade could pet the animals."

Someone else said, "That's dumb. What if an animal bites somebody?"

Sophia waved her hands for calm. When she had their attention, she asked, "Who can tell me what a theme is?" Whitney raised her hand, so she called on her.

"It's the meaning of something like a story, or in this case, it's probably what they want the floats to be decorated like, like if the theme is Christmas trees, then all the floats will probably have Christmas trees on them."

"Oh, can we have a Christmas tree on our float?" Maya asked.

"Yeah," Clevon said, "Because you probably won't have one at home."

Before Sophia or Brittney could say anything to him, Whitney shot him a warning glance and cautioned him, "Don't be mean."

Sophia looked at Britt and whispered under her breath, "Apparently those two are becoming a couple and doing it faster than I thought."

Brittney rolled her eyes. "Just what you need, teenagers in heat," she whispered back.

She refrained from elbowing her friend as she turned her attention back to the kids. "Whitney is right about what a theme is, and this parade has one. The theme is, 'Home for the Holidays' this year."

Everyone looked around at each other. Clevon, as expected, was the first to speak. "What are we gonna do with that?"

"We're glad you asked," Brittney said, stepping in. "We want you each to come up with an idea about what home means to you. So, everybody think about that and write your thought down on one of these pieces of paper. It doesn't have to be anything big. A sentence, or even just a word, will do. And it's private. Write whatever you want."

"Like a house?" DeMarco asked.

Sophia moved toward him as she passed out the papers. "I have pencils if anyone doesn't have one in their book bag." To the ten-year-old she said, "Yes, like a house, if that's how you think of home. But, home can be a lot of things. It can be an apartment. It can be the people that live there. It can be things you have that you love."

"Home isn't just a place. It's where your heart is," Brittney said from the other side of the table.

"Or," Sophia added as she laid a hand on DeMarco's shoulder, "like my dad says, 'Home is where you hang your hat.' That means anywhere you are can be your home, if you believe it is."

The boy looked up at her, his expression pleading, "If I have to move somewhere else, Miss Sophia, can I still be in the parade?"

She gave his shoulder a squeeze. "I'll do my best to get you here as long as you call me and tell me where you are."

The kids worked quietly for a couple minutes. While Brittney helped Maya, Sophia glanced around for Lacie. She spotted her on the far side of the room, texting away on her phone. The grin on her face told her she probably wasn't texting someone at work. *Must be her girlfriend.*

She grimaced, but then shook her head to clear it and focused her attention back on the kids. When they finished writing, they help up their scraps of paper for the two women to collect. Once they had them all, Sophia stood at the head of the table and began reading them off out loud. Will came out of his office to listen.

"Grandma," Sophia called out. *Definitely Clevon's writing.*

"Warm stuff like clothes and blankets," Brittney read from another.

"Lots of food to eat," Sophia read. *This might have been a bad idea. It's breaking my heart.*

"An apartment big enough to have my own room," Brittney read.

It went on like that for a few minutes as the two women read twenty-one slips of paper. When they had read them all, they looked at each other.

Sophia released a heavy breath. "So, okay. What do we do with all of this?"

Lacie called out, "I have an idea."

WHILE THEY WERE all cleaning up, Lacie asked, "Do you have breaks in your class schedule tomorrow where you two could stop by my company before we have to be here?"

"Why?" Sofia had liked Lacie's idea, but she was annoyed at her all the same for not being fully there for the kids and their needs. *I'm not giving in to her that easily.*

Her matter-of-fact answer, "To talk to one of our IT guys," threw her off.

Shoot. She did mention that. I can be such a... I don't even know.

Britt prompted her. "Sophia?"

Sophia sighed. "I'm not sure. Possibly." Then she gave in. "Probably."

"I know it's short notice, but we're kind of in a time crunch here, anyway. I've been texting him for the last hour. He's excited about helping with the float and if anyone can make our idea work, he can."

"Your idea."

"Ours," Lacie said again, with firmness in her voice. "All of ours." She circled a finger in the air. "You two came up with the right question, the kids provided the answers, and I figured out how to put it all together."

"Is this what you do for your actual job?" Brittany asked.

"Actually, yes. It's a part of it. Sometimes things work like they're supposed to." She gave Sofia an elbow tap on the upper arm. "What do you say? Can you come by and help us hash out a plan?"

She looked at her friend. "Britt and I ride into campus

together. My only class tomorrow ends at 11:30. We usually do lunch together, then I take the bus over here. It's not far."

"I have two classes tomorrow," Britt said, "and my second one goes a lot later, which usually works out perfectly for us."

Sophia put in, "She picks me up when I'm done here. I could take the bus to your company instead... if it goes there."

"I'm at Tech Success, in the technology park, southeast of your campus. I'm pretty sure it does."

"Will should be the one to go," Sophia said to Brittney, more than to Lacie. "He's the primary float builder." *I just babysit the kids, basically.*

Lacie must have picked up on her tone. "You're the one who started sketching out a design when I told you my idea," she reminded her. "Have some confidence in yourself. Besides, it's just a one-on-one chat with a guy about your age who's as shy and backward as they come, but he's a whiz with timing apps."

At Sophia's skeptical look, she said, "You know those 4th of July fireworks shows, set to music? My company sponsored Denver's show last year. He worked with Zambelli Fireworks to do all the timed music."

"Wow," Britt said. "That was a great show."

It was. Sophia took a deep breath. "Okay, then, I guess." *Guess I'm meeting you and him outside of here. Oh boy...*

8

AWKWARD MEETUP

Friday, November 15th
Tech Success, Inc.
Denver, Colorado

Lacie paced the little piece of floor alongside her desk, between her front and back cubicle walls. *It's just a meeting. Nobody is going to care.*

She stopped pacing, sat, and tried some relaxation breathing. It didn't help. *Maybe if I sit...* A minute later, she was still on edge. *I don't know why I volunteered everything I did given the reason I'm working at the rec center in the first place. Stupid! Stupid! And now Sofia is coming here, and I'll be introducing her to my coworkers. This is going to blow up in my face, I just know it.*

She heard Kendall speaking to someone else in the open area down from her cube. She jumped up and went to beckon her friend.

Kendall appeared in the opening a minute later. "What's up?"

Lacie waved her in. "Big ears out there. I don't want anyone else to hear this."

Kendall made a show of tiptoeing over to the chair she sometimes occupied and sat down gingerly.

"Very funny."

"Just tell me what's going on, already."

"I've been working at that rec center, right? Well, they're putting a float in Denver's holiday parade, and I sort of volunteered one of our IT guys to help set their lights to music. I'm having a meeting with him in about ten minutes."

"Ted, I bet. He's amazing, a whiz at that stuff. What's the problem?"

"He doesn't know *why* I'm working at the center."

Kendall was matter-of-fact. "Just tell him you're volunteering if it even comes up."

"But we're using company assets."

"Hmm. That could be a problem, but there's got to be a way around that. I mean, we donate things to causes and organizations all the time. Why don't you let me work on that?"

"I just don't want to... "

Kendall waved her off. "Don't say it and don't worry about it, I won't blow your cover."

Lacie breathed a sigh of relief, but then she remembered Sofia. "There's one more thing. Sofia is on her way here to meet with both of us."

"Ah. The love interest."

Lacie hissed through clenched teeth, "I told you, it's not like that!"

"Okay. Okay," Kendall said as she held up her hands.

"I just need you to try to run interference if Heaven gets to wandering around in this area."

She said it a little louder than she intended, and Heaven

rounded the corner to confront her about it. "I'm getting ready to walk by, and I hear my name. What's going on?"

"Unlikely," Kendall said. "How long have you been standing out there listening to our conversation?"

Heaven put her hands on her hips and leaned into Kendall. "I was just walking by, Ms. know it all. Stay out of my business." She turned her ire on Lacie next.

"You said Wednesday night that we'd talk yesterday, then you avoided me all day."

"I had meetings all day, yesterday." *I barely made it out of here on time to get to the center before the kids started showing up.*

Heaven didn't buy it. "What's really going on here?" She flung an arm out toward Kendall. "Why does she need to run interference for me?"

Sweat started to run down Lacie's back. *I don't know what's generating more heat, having three bodies in here, or Heaven's anger.*

Ted showed up in the doorway, smart phone in hand. "Come in," Lacie said when she spied him. "The more the merrier." *Because sarcasm is better than me screaming right now.*

He squeezed past Heaven and stood with his back against the filing cabinet on the wall opposite where Lacie had been pacing. "Are we having our meeting in here?"

Lacie gave him a nod. "Yes, in just a few minutes." She gave Heaven a pointed look. The other woman didn't budge.

Ted looked down at his phone, then up at Kendall and Heaven. "I had that we'd be meeting with a Sophia, but not with these two." It was more a question than a statement, but he continued to stare at the screen on his phone.

Lacie tensed at his awkwardness and at Heaven's immediate response.

"Who's Sophia?"

"She's in charge of the project I'm working on," Lacie managed.

Heaven crossed her arms over her ample chest. Her eyes darted back and forth between Lacie and Ted as she demanded, "From this company?"

"It's the project the company is involved in, yes."

Ted looked confused when he looked up, but he said nothing to contradict her.

Kendall gave Lacie a wink Heaven couldn't see, and then she motioned for Ted to follow her. "Since you have a few minutes yet, Ted, I wonder if you could check out something for me real quick?"

"Um, sure. I guess. Did you put in a work order?" he asked her as he followed her out.

AT HER OWN CUBICLE, Kendall pulled him in by the wrist and explained, "There really isn't a problem with any of my equipment. I just wanted to let you in on something Heaven doesn't know about that she'll make a big deal of because her boss kept her out of the loop."

Ted gave Kendall a sideways look. "Okay, I don't like the sound of this. I think I should just go back down to IT." He took his smart phone back out of his shirt pocket and checked the time.

She waggled a hand at him. "No, no. Don't worry, it's nothing bad at all." She gave him her most winning smile. "It's really good, actually. The company is giving some behind-the-scenes support to the Sun Valley Community Rec Center. Very behind the scenes. It's kind of hard to explain, but they don't want to take any credit for it. It's simply what they call 'Goodwill' for the company, something they can do to help the center and write off on their taxes."

"But why wouldn't they want anyone to know?"

Kendall shrugged. "Beats me. But, if you know Heaven, she'll blab to the moon and the stars and then everyone will know, so it's best we don't talk about it around her. Hopefully, Lacie is dealing with her."

TED WAS CARRYING a chair when he and Kendall returned to Lacie's cubicle.

"I had him bring my extra chair up," Kendall informed Lacie of the obvious from outside the entry way. "You're going to need it." Heaven stepped out so he could carry it into the cubicle.

Kendall saw her chance. "Heaven, if you're done here, why don't you come with me? I have a project you might be able to help me with."

The other woman started to respond, but she stopped mid-sentence and stared down the passageway between cubicles. "I think your 'Sofia' is here. She looks lost."

She's still mad, Lacie thought. *This is going to be bad. So bad.*

"You're looking for Lacie?" Kendall called out to the lone woman.

"Yes."

"Up here."

Sophia approached slowly and looked into the cube as Kendall appraised her and Heaven gave her a stare down she didn't seem to notice because she was focused on Lacie.

Lacie did her best to smile and keep her voice from cracking. "You found me."

"It wasn't too bad getting here. But your security sign-in procedures are pretty strict." She fingered her visitors' badge.

"Sorry about that. I should have warned you." Pointing around the room, Lacie introduced everyone. "That's Ted from IT. He'll be helping us with your plans. That's Kendall Jordan. She's an administrative assistant - the administrative assistant - for all of us senior business analysts here." *Hope this is sounding official.* "She may be giving us some help if she can fit us into her busy schedule." She pointed last at Heaven who was now back to standing just inside the door, making it a tight fit for the four of them and the two chairs squeezed into the area in front of Lacie's desk. "And that's Heaven Walker. She's the Executive Assistant to one of our VP's. She and Kendall were just leaving."

"We are?" Heaven asked. "If we're all going to help, why can't we stay and get up to speed, as you always like to say?"

Lacie saw Sophia wince. She steeled herself and said with all f the courtesy in her tone she could muster, "This is a very preliminary meeting, like I told you a minute ago. My cube is really small and I'm already sweating."

Ted nodded along as she talked.

Heaven turned on a heel and attempted to storm off almost knocking Kendall over in her haste.

Kendall sketched a wave at Sophia and her coworkers and left quietly.

$\sim$

"So, what did you think?" Lacie asked Sofia on the way to the center. "I think we have a great plan."

"It was good," Sophia said.

Lacie sensed her unease. *And I'm pretty sure I know why.* "Don't let Heaven get to you."

"Your girlfriend?"

"She's not my girlfriend."

"Right. For 'not your girlfriend,' she's very possessive of you. You need to tell her I'm no threat to her. No threat at all."

"Anything Heaven and I had is over." *I just haven't told her yet.*

"Does she know that? Wait... don't answer that. It's really none of my business." She stared out her window for a minute, then asked, answer me this, "I passed an empty conference room on the way to your cubicle. If Kendall and Heaven are really going to help us, why couldn't we all meet in there?"

"I... I guess I never thought of it."

"Never thought of it, or is there something you don't want Heaven to know? Or is it me?"

Lacie swallowed, pushing the panic swelling from her stomach into her throat down, then put Sofia's question off by answering, "I'll read both of them in, but Ted, if you didn't notice, is the shy, backward type. I didn't want to throw too much at him. Two on one was enough for him. Anyway, what did you think of his rope light idea?"

"I liked it, but they cost a lot, I'm sure. They'll be hard to divide up after the parade too."

"Don't be so sure. Remember our idea." She waited for Sophia's answering nod before going on. "And, to be frank, I had a pretty good idea that was what he'd suggest, so I've already got the money part of that all worked out. Kendall will help me get enough rounded up or ordered and shipped quick." *I hope. She owes me for getting me into all of this in the first place, after all. I really need to remind her of that.*

"I sure hope so. The kids will be so disappointed if we can't pull this off."

"What about you?"

"What about me?"

"Will you be disappointed?"

"I'm not a kid. I mean, it will be a little sad, but I'll get over it a lot quicker than they will." She bit her lower lip.

Lacie glanced over at her, and noticing that she gave her, her best smile. "Don't worry about a thing. I'm not going to let you or them down." When Sophia didn't respond, she went on, "Let's get the homework and a quick snack taken care of first today, and then let's get the older kids started helping Will to build our base structure."

9

TRUTH TELLING

Saturday Morning, November 16th
Vaca Home
Highlands Ranch, Colorado

S ofia dusted her hands against her jeans after she finished putting hay flakes in each horse stall. Her nose twitched, the dust of the dried hay tickling it into a series of sneezes.

Brittney glanced over from a stall on the other side of the barn where she was brushing down a mare. "I really think you're allergic to hay."

"No." Sophia shook her head as she sneezed twice more. "I'm allergic to dust. Any dust. Mama keeps such a clean house, I'm extra sensitive when I come out here."

"I haven't heard you say that in years."

"About dust?"

"Mama. You never call her that."

Sofia shrugged.

"Have you tried talking to her about how you feel?"

"Feel about what?"

"Come on, Sofia. You know what I'm talking about."

"Britt, if this is about Lacie, drop it, okay?"

"She who protests... "

"I said drop it!" She turned her back on her friend and walked to the other end of the barn.

Brittney put the brushes away and followed. She found Sofia sitting outside in the cold on an old wire spool. "I'm sorry." She leaned against the spool next to her friend and waited.

"I don't know anything about her, Britt. I'm doing my best to keep my distance and keep it that way. She's only here for a little while. After the holidays, she'll be gone, and life will go on."

"And if she decides to stick around? What will you do then? You can't hide from any feelings you may be having forever."

"I don't know what I feel."

"You're interested in her. Anyone with eyes can see that."

She gave in, "Anyone who cares to see it, but no one really cares but you. I can admit it to you. It doesn't matter anyway, because she's not interested in me. How could she be? I'm half her age, half her height and I have about a quarter of her life experience."

"She is interested in you. Just like I can see it in you, I can see it in her. And, I can tell your mother sees it too."

"Mama treated her like crap the other night."

"Not exactly true. She was aloof, in her usual way with newcomers, but your dad likes her. That should count for something."

"It might... if there were something there for us, but there's not. I think you're wrong about her."

"No. I'm not. You're carrying your baggage with your mother.

I don't know what baggage she has but I can see she's pretty wrapped up in her work."

Sofia shook her head slowly. "Baggage? I'll tell you; she has a girlfriend, for one. Who knows what else? Like I said, I don't know much about her. I don't even know how she came to us. It's all a little odd."

"You didn't ask her?"

"Yes... no, not directly. I assumed she was a volunteer and she said she was."

"I don't understand. What's the problem?"

"Usually when we get a new staff member, even a volunteer, they have to have a background check and we're told they're coming long before they show up. We work with kids, after all. It's protocol and that protocol is based on rules and common sense. In her case, she just showed up one day."

"You don't think she came through the proper channels?"

"I can't answer that. She may have, but I haven't been told anything. Maybe I should run a court docket search on her."

"You don't think there's something criminal there, do you? She seems so put together. Besides, why would Will—"

Sophia stopped her. "You're right. What am I thinking? Will wouldn't do anything to put any of our kids in danger. That's not like him at all."

Brittney touched her friend on the shoulder. "I have to tell you, while we were figuring out the build on top of the trailer last night and she was working with the younger kids, I overhead some things."

She panicked all over again. "Like what?"

"Relax. Nothing bad. It's just, she was asking each of the little ones what they want for Christmas... what they really want, if they could have anything at all and anything that cost something besides money."

Sophia let out the breath she'd been holding and managed a small smile. "That second part is my influence at work." She stood. "I'm curious; did you hear any of the answers?"

"A few. Maya's was cute and a total surprise. She wants to ride a horse."

Sophia looked back over her shoulder at the barn. "Now that, I could probably arrange."

SHE SAT IN THE WINDOW, staring out into the waning light. She could hear her mother in the kitchen banging pots and pans around. She knew she should help get dinner on the table. *I just can't face her right now. She's standing in the way of what I really want, a real relationship. One where I'm an equal. One with someone who feels the same about me as I feel about her. A relationship with a woman who loves me for me, no matter what. A relationship with someone sure of herself and sure of what she wants... someone like Lacie.*

Lacie. She's all I've thought about for the past few days. What if Britt is right? She can't be right... can she?

She didn't hear her dad come in. She wasn't aware he had been watching her until his hand touched her shoulder and she jumped.

"I didn't mean to scare you. It just looked like you were so lost in thought. Need to talk?" Hector asked his youngest child.

Sofia pursed her lips and shook her head.

He gave her a moment to gather herself, then he said, "You know you can tell me anything. *Anything*. You're my daughter. The flesh of my flesh. You could never disappoint me."

She closed her eyes and inhaled. *If only it were that easy.* She opened her eyes and looked at him. "Do you love Mama?" she asked.

A smile spread across his face. "You really have to ask?"

"Yes. It's just... It seems like... I'm not sure how to say this so I'm just going to say it; It seems like she's not your equal. She serves you in the traditional old ways. I... I can't ever see myself doing that."

He shook his head quickly, side to side. "No, no. You've got it all wrong. We do for each other. We always have. Your mother, she does what she loves. I do everything in my power to see that she can do it. If she wants the best cut of meat to make our dinner, the ripest tomatoes, whatever it is, I find a way to make sure she gets what she wants, what she needs. She doesn't find cooking for me - for any of her family - a chore, a service. It's one of the great joys of her life. Long after you go to bed at night on Friday nights, she sits up going through her mother's recipe box, through her own recipes, her cookbooks, what have you planning for us. That's just one example. Ask her if you don't believe me."

"I do, Dad. I knew about her planning. I always thought she was trying to figure out the best way to stretch out the money."

"In that case, you were wrong." He took her hand and rubbed his thumb over her palm. "We've never wanted you or your sister to do without. We've always been very careful with money, both of us. It was our decision. A joint decision. We did it for you two and for our grandchildren. Sending you both to school. Giving Concetta a nice wedding. Making sure those kids of hers have what they need."

"Starting out in marriage is such a struggle. Your sister is taken care of, because that's what she's chosen, but we help because we want the best for her and her family. We want the best for you too, whatever you decide."

She tried to read his face, but he turned from her. "Come on. The banging around stopped. Dinner must be about ready."

· · ·

SHE SAT up in her bed that night, wide awake, thinking about what her father said. *He knows. He knows who I really am and he's okay with it. Oh... but what is mama thinking?*

10

LIGHTS

Sunday Morning, November 17th
Greenwood Village

L acie scrolled again through all the choices at the Christmas lighting site. She and Kendall had gone back and forth on Skype as they pored over lighting options for more than an hour. When Kendall had to hang up to take care of some personal business, she left Lacie with two great choices to decide between.

Rather than decide, Lacie immediately started to second guess their picks. With no one to bounce her thoughts off of, she couldn't bring herself to make a final commitment to purchase.

She thought of Sophia. *She'd probably know what to do... what to pick that the kids would love.* She couldn't call her. She never thought to get her number. *How would I explain what I'm doing, anyway?*

She realized then, she needed to step up. She steeled herself and checked both of the best options one more time. She flicked over to her bank account link and logged in. She didn't need to survey her account. She was aware of the total of her funds in checking and savings with the bank. The money was there. *The cause is worthy.*

Reassured, she went with the slightly more expensive package of lights, splitters, and connectors she knew would work for Sophia and Ted's design. She wanted to be sure they had everything they needed. She selected rush, early AM shipping for Tuesday at more than double the cost of three-to-five-day ground shipping, swallowed her tendency to be tight with her money unless she knew the exact return on investment or the life expectancy of an item, and paid the nearly $900.00 tab.

As she pulled her receipt off her printer, she thought again about Sophia. *It doesn't matter what I should be doing. It doesn't matter that she's only twenty-two. I want her. I only want her. As bad as I want to stay away and let her work things out on her own. As bad as I need to focus on myself and my career, I'm so drawn to her.*

She sighed. *If I'm ever going to have any chance with her at all, I'm going to have to come clean and tell her why I'm working at the rec center in the first place.*

Her thoughts drifted to her community service hours. She pulled the calendar up on her phone and ran some calculations. She realized she wasn't going to meet the requirements of her sentence at her current pace of about fifteen hours a week. *And I'm exhausted. I can't keep up another month and a half of thirteen to fourteen-hour days, Monday through Friday even though it won't get me where I need to be at the end of the year. Either Judge Hildalgo is going to have to be more flexible with me, or I'm going to have to find more time to document.* She thought of finding a place where she could work over the weekends instead of knocking out two to three hours at a time, but anywhere else she went wouldn't include Sophia. *That's not what I want either.*

Her phone buzzed on the desk next to her. She checked the

text. 'Heaven,' she said out loud. The other woman had gone to the Friday night concert with a friend after their standoff in the office that morning. Lacie figured she must have drunk herself silly because she drunk dialed her after 2:00 AM Saturday morning. When she begged off going over there as Heaven drifted in and out of sleep over the phone, she knew for sure she'd have to end it. She knew she needed to break it off with her once and for all. *I just hope that she doesn't make waves at work...*

Her mind shifted from Heaven to the kids at the center. It's funny, she thought to herself. *I never wanted kids of my own, but I'm starting to have a real soft spot for several of them. They make me laugh. DeMarco makes me want to cry. I don't know how Sophia can detach herself from some of their realities... I could never be a social worker.*

She chuckled. *They always stop me in my tracks when I get to thinking more about costs and making money than about what will make them happy. Sofia too.*

Powerful feelings overcame her. She realized she wanted to do right by all of them, give them a good Christmas. Dozens of thoughts sprang to mind. Several minutes later, as she tried to come up with a plan she could present to Will and Sophia she started to worry that she might be overstepping the wants of the kids' families. *I don't want to do that, but how do I get their families involved, too?*

She thought of little Maya, and she wondered if she could get Sophia to arrange for her to ride a horse at the ranch where her dad managed the stables. Hector seemed very civic-minded. Sophia had told her all about his influence on her chosen path. *I think we can swing that wish, as long as Hector's boss doesn't have any heartburn with it. Maybe I can ride with her. Her, and Sophia.* She thought back on growing up with her mother and grand-mother in Oklahoma. She'd spent a lot of time - some of her only happy times - on horseback. *It's been years. Too many years. I miss it.*

~

"THE LIGHTS ARE ORDERED, and they shipped today," Lacie told Will and Sophia. "They'll be here tomorrow."

Will gave her a raised eyebrow appraisal. "Wow. That's quick!"

"We don't have a lot of time."

"I meant to raise the money."

"Um... what can I say. My company was feeling pretty generous." She tried to read his expression to see if he was onto her lie, but he had already turned away, rubbing his hands in a gleeful gesture. "Guess the kids and I need to get this puppy finished and painted tonight then so we can start working on that part tomorrow."

Sophia, who'd hardly spoken in the five minutes she'd been there, finally piped up, "How d'you do it?"

I'm going to tell her. I'm going to tell her. "It's a long story. I'll explain it all later, but right now we have to get ready for the kiddos."

"Did you buy them?"

"I promise to explain everything."

"You did buy them, didn't you? Why would you do that?"

Will called out something about trying to find a certain paint, interrupting, giving Lacie some precious time to figure out how to frame her approach.

· · ·

"WILL your IT guy be here tomorrow?" Sophia asked Lacie as they set up a craft project for the little kids that would become part of the float decorations when it was complete.

"Probably not. It's kind of short notice since I didn't get the shipment confirmation until just before I left work today, but I'll see if he can be here Wednesday. And, speaking of the lights, I may be a few minutes late tomorrow. I'll have to get all the stuff loaded and over here." *After I pick it up at my condo association office.*

"Is it a lot?"

"I'd say so. A couple of big boxes with spools of rope lights for sure and at least one other box with some other stuff to cut and splice and connect and who knows what all else. It's all the stuff Ted told us to order."

"Well, that front slot should be open. I can put something there to make sure it is, and Will and Clevon can help lug it all in."

"I'll call down and talk to Ted tomorrow, get his schedule. In the meantime, we can probably unpack everything and lay it out, start figuring out how we're going to do what we want to do."

Sophia gave the kids some basic instruction on the art project, then turned back to Lacie. "We all need to get together and start talking about the Holiday party too. This is the most urgent thing right now, but that will be on us before we know it."

Lacie waved a hand toward the kids. "You and I can talk now, if it's okay to talk in front of them."

"About the basic stuff, we can." She appeared to think for a minute and then started in. "I think I told you, we do it Christmas Eve. Is that going to be a problem for you to be here?"

"No, not at all." *I'm all alone in the world.*

"No plans with family?"

"No." When she realized Sofia was waiting for more, she said, "It's a long story. My father left when I was really young, and my mother didn't have a lot to do with raising me. My grandmother did. She died a while back."

Sophia visibly winced. "I'm so sorry. No other family?"

Lacie shook her head no as she answered, "I have two half-brothers I haven't seen in years. They're my father's boys from his second marriage. I was never close to him, and I barely know them."

"That's so sad."

No, it isn't. I'm past it all now.

"Family is so important, but that's the kind of story I hear all the time around here, unfortunately. And, it's the sort of story I imagine I'm going to hear for my whole career as a social worker."

Lacie could only nod in agreement to that.

Sophia blew out a breath. "Enough about that... I mean, not to minimize your experience, but we really do need to talk about the party."

"Let's look at it from my perspective as an outsider looking in. What do I see?"

"Food."

"Okay."

"Some sort of entertainment. Usually, we have a DJ or a small group that gets together and plays Christmas carols and everyone sings along."

"Okay."

"We already talked about the kids doing a show this year instead... but I'm not sure how all of that would. When we used to have them do that in the past, but that was when we had more staff to work with them and put something together."

"I'll help. Brittney said she'd help."

"And she will, but she's got school and a job at the ranch, and she's planning her own wedding... "

Lacie raised a hand. "Okay, let's table that idea for a minute. What else?"

Sophia bent over the table to help one of the boys with the glue then said, "Small presents for everyone, like Britt and I were telling you last week." That got a reaction around the table.

Giving a thumbs up, Lacie said, "Okay, on the presents."

"Santa." A cheer rose up from the kids around the table when Sophia mentioned him.

"Um... I don't know about Santa," Lacie said.

Faces fell.

"Has everyone here actually been good this year? Or, have you all been a bunch of little misfits?"

A couple of kids asked at the same time, "What's a misfit?"

Sophia shot Lacie a look. "I think you should take that one."

"A misfit is... You're David, right?" she asked one of the youngsters that posed the question.

"Yep. David. That's me."

"Well, David, a misfit is someone that... someone that doesn't... Someone who doesn't—"

Sophia took pity on Lacie and came to her rescue. "It's a word we use sometimes when someone doesn't fit in. Ms. Lacie was trying to use it to say some of us may not have been very good this year in the eyes of Santa Claus."

"So, she used the word wrong," David said in a matter-of-fact tone.

Lacie couldn't help her mirth. "Yes, I did!" she said as she chuckled.

When the kids had all focused back on their projects, Lacie and Sophia moved a little way away to continue their conversation.

"Sorry about that," Lacie said.

"Don't worry about it. It was cute."

"Cute on them, or cute watching me struggle to explain?"

"Both."

"We talked about some of that stuff before. What I really need to ask you about is funding and costs."

"Will has the actual figures of what we have on hand from a financial perspective. I have a basic idea. We have the party here, of course, so there's no added expense there. We do usually have to rent some tables and chairs because what you see out there is what we have."

"Ouch. I hadn't thought of that. How much do you think?"

"When the church down the street lets us borrow theirs, it's just the finding help and vehicles to haul them up here and back. Last year they had a program on Christmas Eve, so we couldn't use them. The rental then was over $200.00."

"Double ouch. We better get in touch with the church soon. If we can't get them, we'll have time to search for some other options."

Sophia nodded. "We've had a DJ who played free for us in the past, even though it was Christmas Eve. That was okay, but it's not really a dancing crowd. It's pretty much eating, sing a few songs, then Santa visits and we do the gifts. The expense is in the food, tableware, decorations, and the gifts. Last year we had almost two hundred people eat. We spent nearly $1,000.00 in food and table service."

"Wait, where on earth do you cook that much food?"

"We don't. We can't," Sophia admitted. "We buy the food, and a caterer donates time to cook it, bring it in, and set it up."

"For two-hundred people? Wow! That's generous."

"Her and her husband are long-time supporters of the center. He immigrated here with his parents. They both grew up in Sun Valley and made it out, real local success stories. They do it to give back to the community. You might have heard of them; Hildalgo Catering? That's her company, and he's a Common Pleas Court judge in the county."

"Oh." Lacie could feel the beads of sweat forming on her forehead.

DILEMMA

Tuesday Morning, November 19th
Tech Success, Inc.
Denver, Colorado

L acie haunted the hallway outside of her cubicle as she
waited for Kendall. When her friend finally showed up
for work, on time for her usual start time, she
rushed her.

Kendall gave her an exasperated look. "Really? What is so
important that you've sent me three texts already this morning
and tried to call me twice?"

"We need to talk... I need to talk to you ASAP."

"Can it wait another minute while I get a cup of coffee?" She
picked her mug up off her desk.

"Yes, and I'll walk to the break room with you. I don't want to
talk in here."

"Let me guess," Kendall whispered, leaning in close, "it's
something you don't want Heaven to overhear if she's hovering?"

Lacie gave her a single dip of the head in response.

As they walked to the break room, Kendall asked, "I thought you were going to break off your little dalliance with her?"

"I was... I am. I'm going to do that really soon, but that's not what's important right now."

While Kendall waited for a mocha coffee to brew from one of the line of Keurig machines on the counter, Lacie told her about Judge Hildalgo being a supporter of the center.

Kendall took her cup from the machine and held it to her nose. "Ah." She took a sip and savored it. "It's not coffee shop good, but it's the best mocha out there for these babies." She looked back at one of the machines wistfully.

"Could you focus on something besides your coffee for a minute? I have a real problem here."

"I don't see it like that."

"Pardon?"

"You were going to tell Sophia anyway, right?" When Lacie didn't respond, she prompted her again, "Right?"

"Yes. I planned to."

"It seems to me that would have been the perfect opportunity."

"I couldn't think straight. She... her telling me that took me by total surprise."

"Okay, so tell her tonight."

"Do you think that's a good idea? Maybe I just let the whole thing go... just forget it."

Kendall stayed quiet for a minute, leaving her to her thoughts.

Lacie knew when she was beaten. "I have to tell her, don't I?"

"If I were in your place, I would. It's not my call though." She stepped away from the counter and moved toward the door.

As she followed behind, Lacie asked, "He set me up, didn't he?"

"The judge? I hardly think he was trying to get you a hookup by sending you there," Kendall said as Lacie drew alongside her in the hall.

"Shh! And, sarcasm does not become you. You know what I meant. He sent me there for a reason."

"He sure did. They needed help, and he sent it to them. It's as simple as that."

Lacie sighed. "It blows up my other plan."

"What was that?"

"I was going to go back and ask him to reduce my time. At best, I'm getting fifteen hours a week at Sun Valley. There's no way I'm going to finish the time I—" She realized she was about to divulge how careless she'd been about her sentence, and she looked down at her feet as they rounded the corner into the area they and many of their coworkers referred to not so fondly as cubeville.

"You're cute when you're embarrassed. You were saying?"

She came clean. "I owed a lot more hours than I let on to you a couple of weeks ago. He wanted me to finish them by the end of the year."

"Ah." She put her free hand on Lacie's shoulder and leaned in. "Do you think he figured you wouldn't be able to, but he was banking on them using you every second they could?"

LACIE TEXTED Sophia and asked to meet her for lunch, just the two of them.

Lacie: I have something I need to tell you, and something to ask you.

Sophia: Can it wait until we get to the center?

Lacie debated her response, then typed, No, not really.

Sophia: Can we meet near campus?

Lacie did a quick Google search then typed, Sure. Sandwiches at Cheba Hut?

Sophia: It'll be packed with students at lunch.

Sophia: How about Which Wich in the con center? And, there's parking.

Lacie: Deal. Meet you at noon.

SHE PUT in for four hours of personal time and left at 10:00 AM without waiting around to see if anyone approved it or even noticed. After a detour home to pick up the lights, she drove over to the convention center and found parking near the entrance closest to the interior food court.

THEY WAITED in a line snaking toward the counter to order their sandwiches with Lacie shepherding Sofia along in front of her. *It's a lot more crowded in here than I bargained for.*

The young man in line in front of Sofia looked back at her then elbowed his buddy ahead of him as Lacie watched. She couldn't hear what he said, but from the other man's laughter, she gathered it was something crude.

The first man turned back to Sofia and bent at the neck to compensate for her much shorter height to talk to her. Lacie couldn't quite pick up what he said to Sofia either, but she seemed to take it well, replying with something that had him nodding.

When he straightened, Lacie caught his eye and gave him her best hands-off look.

He glanced back down at Sofia, dipped his head in acknowledgment of whatever had passed between them, then turned back to his buddy.

Lacie bent much as he had, but she spoke into Sofia's ear from over her left shoulder. "I think you have an admirer." *Or someone looking for a quick fling.* "He was really flirting."

Sofia turned to her, mirth in her eyes, and said, "Not hardly, unless he's really bad at it. He said I reminded him of a young version of his little Italian Nonna."

Lacie managed to hold in her own laughter. "Well then, that's kind of a back-handed compliment." *He needs some new lines, but not to use on this one.*

"Ted said he could come tomorrow and show us what to do to get the lights started."

Sofia wasn't going to let her drag the real reason for their impromptu lunch out. As she unwrapped her sub, she asked, "So, what did you need to tell me?"

Lacie coughed on the swig of soda she'd just taken. When she regained her composure, she said, "There were two things, actually. One of them, I'm not sure I want to talk about in here. It's a lot more crowded than I thought it might be."

"There's a convention going on. Who would have thought it in the middle of November?" She dropped the sarcasm when she saw Lacie's face and asked instead, "Do you want to wait and talk about it at the center?"

She focused on unwrapping her own sub and not meeting Sophia's eyes as she said, "No. I need to tell you this." *I'll just clean it up for anyone listing in.* She took a bite, chewed, swallowed, then plunged ahead. "I got in some minor legal trouble over the summer," she mumbled as she glanced upward to see if Sophia had heard.

"Um, okay... "

"I'm telling you because it's the real reason I'm working at the center." She looked up and met Sophia's big brown eyes with her own.

"What sort of legal trouble?" the younger woman asked, the tone of a social worker - in training or not - emanating in her voice.

"It was nothing, really, but I got some community service time that I have to do. Your Judge Hildalgo patron sent me to you, to Sun Valley."

Sofia skipped right over that. "So, you're telling me you're technically on probation for something and that's why—"

"No." She shook her head vigorously. "No jail time. No probation. Very low-level misdemeanors that—"

Sophia's voice got a little louder. "Anything that would affect you being able to work with kids?"

"No. I swear. Nothing like that."

The younger woman leaned in and whispered, "No sex offender registry?"

"No." *Thank God!* She could feel sweat running down her back. She forced out a smile and took a small sip of her drink.

Sophia stared at her, then she smiled back. "You're putting me on, then."

"No."

"You are. Will would have said something."

"Hildalgo talked to him right before I first showed up there and got knocked on my ass... as I recall." The memory made them both chuckle, but she stopped laughing first. "I don't know what all he told him, but Will does know. I'm actually surprised he didn't tell you."

"Yeah. Me too." She eyed Lacie. "Are you going to tell me what you did?"

"Why don't you just ask Will that?"

"Because I still don't know whether to believe you. You seem so... so—"

"So what?"

"Sincere. So put together. It's hard to believe you got in any sort of trouble that got you arrested and convicted."

"I agree. I was stupid. A momentary lapse in judgement I deeply regret." *And I'm probably going to pay for it in guilt, at a minimum, for the rest of my life.*

"What else?"

Lacie stopped her sub mid-way to her mouth. "Come again?"

"You said you needed to tell me something and ask me something. I assume that's what you wanted to tell me, so what do you want to ask me?"

"And you're okay with what I've told you?"

Sophia rocked back on her chair; hands spread. "I don't know enough to know what to think. I'm still not sure I believe you."

"It's true, and I'm not proud of it. Here's the thing and it ties together with what I want to ask you. See, my company doesn't know anything about it, and I'd prefer to keep it that way."

"Hmm. You say it's minor, nothing for us to worry about with the kids we serve, but your company isn't in on the big secret. I'm not in on it—"

It did not surprise her Sophia didn't buy it and she tried to backpedal, "It's... it's embarrassing, okay? I will say that. And, the fact is, there's a guy retiring early next year," *who's only a few years older than me*, "and I'm in line for his vice president spot."

"And you won't get the promotion if your company knows?"

"Possibly not. Probably not. There's no way to be sure."

"I see. Well, I won't tell anyone. I mean, we'll see Ted, but he's hardly the chatty, gossiping type."

We're getting off track. "Keeping it quiet is not what I wanted to ask you, though. I wanted to ask you to come to a company pre-holiday party with me, this Saturday."

Sophia blanched a paler shade of her naturally sun-kissed coloring.

"Not as a date," Lacie corrected.

"Oh." She wouldn't meet Lacie's eyes.

Lacie put her cup down as she waved a hand, drawing the younger woman's gaze back up. "This is coming out all wrong. I meant more for networking. We have a corporate event we do every year before Thanksgiving instead of just before Christmas. I think if I can get you in there to talk to some of our folks, we can get the company involved in helping with the center, helping with the big holiday party and the gifts."

"But... I guess, I thought... isn't your company already involved?"

"Not really."

Sophia gave her a side eye look. "Ted? Kendall? The lights?"

"That was all me," she admitted. "I asked them personally for their help and, what you tried to get me to admit before, I paid for the lights." She felt a weight lift as she admitted that.

"Is paying for stuff part of your community service?" Her tone was angry.

And the weight comes right back. "No. Honestly, I did that because I wanted to. We have policies and procedures at my company and... well, you needed the lights sooner rather than later to get started on your float." She took a deep breath. "I've been chatting with the kids. They've got some pretty extensive wishes. Will told me there's enough in the kitty to cover the food and a few decorations, like you and I talked about, but not much more. My company may help, but I'm not sure how to present it."

"Because you haven't revealed to anyone anything about the center or why you're spending your time there."

It wasn't a question. Lacie hung her head. *She's so perceptive.*

"Why not just ask Will to go? He's the one who knows what

you've done. Ask him to keep it on the down low. Besides, he'll be the one there long after I'm gone."

Lacie's head shot up. "Where are you going?"

"I told you, I graduate at the break. I've got to find a paying job... a good-paying job and get to work on getting my master's. It's time for me to fly on my own."

She misunderstood. "You'd leave the ranch too?"

"It's time for me to carry my own weight. That's what I meant." Sophia stood; her sandwich forgotten. "Come by and talk to him tonight. I'm sure he'd be happy to play your little corporate game."

Lacie jumped up too and followed Sophia outside. "Wait. Let's talk. I promise, I'll tell you everything, but you have to promise not to laugh."

Sophia stopped and looked Lacie over, then gave in. "I'll listen, but no promises."

12

CLEANUP

They sat in Lacie's Outback in the convention center parking lot. Lacie started the car and turned the heat on, but when an initial blast of cool air hit them in the face, she reached over and turned the dial down. "Sorry."

Sophia looked at the clock on the dash. "We have a little bit of time, but I think you better start talking." She waited while the other woman took a deep breath and launched into her story.

"My fortieth birthday was this past summer. I... I've been all about my career for a long time. I wasn't dating anyone; I wasn't planning on doing anything. Kendall had other ideas. We've been friends for a few years now. She insisted I come out with her, her wife, and a few of their friends after work. It was a Friday night; I had no plans. I went. Let's just say, what started out as a nice night out with a few women turned sour a few hours later."

"You got drunk and got picked up for DUI?"

"No. Well, not the DUI part. My birthday is in July. It was blistering hot that day and into the evening. The bar was packed with bodies, the air conditioning couldn't keep up. The frozen margaritas they kept putting in front of me tasted great... couldn't taste the tequila. Bad. I had so many."

"It was so hot. We left the bar, went to some lake. It wasn't far out of the city, but I couldn't tell you where. I didn't recognize it." She lifted a shoulder in a half shrug of lost memory. "Someone bought a bunch of beer along the way." She wagged a finger at Sofia, "Don't ever mix tequila and beer."

"Noted and not a problem. I don't drink."

"Sorry. I'm not trying to tell you what to do. Just a caution. Anyway, long story short, we were all very drunk except a couple of people who were driving. The cops showed up and tried to chase us off."

"Cops?"

"Rangers, actually, I think. We uh... I think we were in a state park."

"And you wouldn't leave?"

"I, um, I might have gotten a little belligerent."

Sofia studied her for several long seconds, then she shook her head and made to get out of the car.

"Where are you going?"

"My car, and then to the center."

"It's still early, Sofia."

"And you're still holding back, Lacie." *She's not telling me everything, for whatever reason.* "I'm done."

Lacie reached out and touched her arm. "Wait. Please."

Sophia turned in the seat. "There was a time when the center had equipment and instructors and served adults too. They had bigger problems than you have, and I learned a few things along the way, like there's no public intoxication statute in Colorado. So, you weren't driving drunk, and you didn't get cited for being drunk in public, then what was it?"

Lacie mumbled something under her breath.

"What was that? I didn't hear you?"

She looked up at Sofia. "I feel like I'm a teenager back in Oklahoma with my grandmother quizzing me about where I've been and what I've been doing."

"I don't mean to lay a guilt trip on you. I just want the truth."

"Okay. Okay." She blew out a breath. "We were skinny dipping." She rushed on to say, "It was so hot, we all just peeled and jumped in the water."

A picture formed in Sofia's mind, and she shifted uncomfortably in her seat. A warmth spread through her core and down her loins. *No, block it out of your mind. Block it out.* "So, you... you got arrested for that?"

"Public indecency, resisting arrest and... assault on a police officer."

"Come again?"

Lacie's face colored crimson. "The resisting arrest and assault charges were dropped."

"Why were you charged with them in the first place?"

"They were fighting with me to get me out of the water... I was drunk but I was lucid enough to be embarrassed. That's why I got resisting arrest."

"And the assault?"

She turned away and mumbled again.

"I couldn't hear what you said."

"I said, I peed on a cop's shoes."

"You what?" Sophia started to laugh. "You're so strait-laced!"

She grimaced. "I haven't been called straight in a really long time." With that, she started to laugh, too. Every time they looked at each other, the laughing began again.

"I just... I can't even imagine that," Sophia managed to get out.

Lacie stopped laughing. "It's funny now, but then it was... it is so embarrassing to me. I assure you; I've never done anything like I did that night. And the sad fact is, I don't remember most of it. Only what Kendall told me and what came out of the police report."

Sophia sobered. "I have to ask again, since you were found guilty of the public indecency—"

"Actually, I plead no contest."

"Okay, so since you were sentenced based on the public indecency, did you have to register as a sex offender?" *I'm not sure I want to know the answer.*

"No, like I said before, and you can check. It was my first and only offense - after they dropped the other charges - and staying off of the list was the primary reason I got as much community service time as I did. I swear to you." She held up her right hand to punctuate her statement.

Sophia waited a few beats before admitting, "I believe you."

"Because you're so trusting."

"No. Because I believe you have some integrity in your soul, you're just embarrassed. You've come clean about paying for things out of your pocket, and now this." She turned as far sideways in the seat as she could manage to be face to face with Lacie. "There's one more thing you need to do."

"I know. I've been trying to hold back, but I can't." She leaned toward Sophia, put a hand on her shoulder, and pulled her into a kiss.

Surprised, Sophia sat there at first, unmoving, then leaned in. Lacie's kiss was tender and sweet, and nothing like she'd experienced in the hurried, stolen moments she'd had with her only girlfriend in her first year of college. She gave in to the sensation.

When Lacie increased the pressure, Sophia moaned and melted against her. As she responded, she felt goosebumps form on her arms, even through the warmth of her coat.

Lacie's hand traveled from Sophia's shoulder, through the softness of her long, dark tresses, down to the small of her back.

She pressed against the bulk of her winter wear, trying to pull her closer.

Sophia shivered at the firmness and insistence of the touch and pulled away. *We can't do this.* She took a deep breath. "I think you misunderstood me."

Lacie looked confused.

"If you want me to come to that party, you need to tell your company. That's what I meant."

She jerked back, the moment of tenderness gone, her reaction instant. "Sophia, no. I can't. I've worked so hard."

13

CONFLICT

S ophia fretted all the way to the center. *She kissed me. I kissed her back.* She put a hand to her face and felt the heat she already knew was there. *We can't... I can't, and there's no way I can go to that party with her now. What am I going to do?*

She knew she was running early, but she was relieved to see the front parking spot was open. She steered into it, shut the car off and sat staring into space. *I don't know what to do.* She thought of Brittney. *She'll know.* She looked at the time on her phone and punched in the speed dial code for her best friend.

When Britt answered, Sophia asked, "Where are you?"

"The stables, why?"

"Is my dad anywhere around?"

"Nope. Just me. He's out riding fence with a couple of the hands."

She breathed a sigh of relief. "Good. I need to talk to you."

"Are you okay? You sound upset."

Her voice shook as she answered, "I don't know. I don't know."

"Calm down. Deep breath."

Sofia did as she was told, drawing in a ragged breath.

"Again."

"I'm okay Britt, and I don't have a lot of time." She drew another breath anyway, then launched into her story with "Lacie kissed me."

"Wait. What?"

"You heard me."

"Okay. How... where—"

"She asked me to lunch to talk to me about something... " She trailed off then, not wanting to divulge a confidence. "Let's just say our discussion got a little bit heated. We took it outside. I was trying to ask her to do one thing and she thought I meant something else, and—"

A tap on her window startled her, causing her to jump and drop her phone. She looked to her left to see Lacie making a motion for her to roll down the window.

She put it down as she fished around between her feet for her phone.

"We need to talk," Lacie said.

She raised a finger, asking her to wait as she put the phone back to her ear. Britt was saying, "Sophia? Sophia, are you there?"

She responded, "Sorry dad. Something startled me. I'll take care of it when I get home tonight." She hated to lie in front of Lacie, something she'd just called her out for, but she didn't want her to think she'd been giving up her secrets.

Lacie backed up so she could get out of the car. "Let's talk out here, in public."

"Sofia... I'm sorry. I apologize from the bottom of my heart. I... I just thought... I don't know what I thought, and it doesn't matter."

Sofia wanted to reach out to her, but she held her ground.

"There are a few things you need to understand. I'm not looking for a relationship, and you're in one."

Lacie closed her eyes and stretched her neck from side to side. "I'm breaking it off with her. I mean that. It was never a real relationship to begin with."

"She thinks so."

"Yes. You're right, she does," Lacie admitted.

"That doesn't change things with us. And, you can't keep on keeping secrets from your company, either. If you want to advance, you have to be honest at work. Bottom line."

"I know. I honestly don't know what I was thinking. C.Y.A. I guess."

"Yeah, well, I've always been taught that honesty—"

"Is the best policy. You're right." Lacie sighed. "I'm going to talk to Heaven first. I'm going to tell her there is no us."

Sophia reached out to her, taking a hold of her arm. "You don't have to do that. Not if you're hoping for... for something between us. I can't... it's not... "

Lacie put a hand over Sophia's and gave the younger woman's hand a squeeze. "I'm not being fair to her, so it's the right thing to do." She drew in a deep breath. "Tomorrow, I'm going to talk to my company. I'll tell them everything, and I'll ask for help for the center because that's also the right thing to do."

Forgetting her trepidation, Sophia smiled broadly and moved to embrace the older woman.

A car sped down the street and stopped halfway between Sophia's parked car and the next one up. Startled, the two women parted but remained close, their bodies still touching.

The passenger window lowered, revealing a glowering Heaven in the driver's seat. "Special company project, huh? Some project! I should have known you were a two-timing ass, Lacie Lindly!"

"Heaven, it's not... "

"Save it! I don't want to hear your excuses! I'll say this though, if you've got the company involved in something without authorization, you're going to regret it." With that, she tromped on the gas and sped away in peel of tires on the cracked pavement.

Sophia looked up at Lacie, stricken. "She... she followed you. Why... how?"

Lacie lifted one shoulder in a half shrug.

"You should probably go and follow her."

"Why?"

"She's got the wrong idea, and—"

"And I was going to break it off with her, anyway. I'm just sorry she thinks you're in the middle of it."

"What if she's been following you all day? She might have seen... seen us... "

"Kiss?"

"Yes." Her spine tingled with the memory. *Lock it up. Push it away.*

"She's still got the wrong impression. You've made that very clear, and I can make it clear to her."

She couldn't suppress the shudder the tingling wrought. "I'm more worried about you than about me. What about your company? She's so mad. What if she goes and blabs everything?"

Lacie reached out to Sophia, taking a hold of her upper arms, turning her toward her again in a loose embrace. "She doesn't know about my personal... er, issue; only that I'm doing something that involves you and Ted. I haven't used any company assets for anything... yet."

"Lacie—"

"Relax. I'll go in tomorrow and do what a good business analyst does. I'll assess the situation, apprise management, and make recommendations. It'll all be fine."

Says you. Sophia's eyes betrayed her.

"I promise." She met her eyes and held them for several seconds until Sophia dropped her gaze. Lacie let go. "Now, we have lights to unload, unpack, and get some order to if we want to get Ted over here and kick this float into high gear." She pointed at Sofia's car. "Can I ask you to switch me spots?"

CLEVON PUT his hands out and swiveled his hips, modeling the old tool belt he'd found in the storeroom. The lone tool in the belt, a small ball peen hammer swung against the leg of his tracksuit. "How do I look?" He waggled his eyebrows suggestively at Whitney.

"Like a fool," Nelda answered instead. "Besides, what you gonna do with that hammer? It won't do anything for those," she said as she pointed at the two spools of lights.

He hopped up on the back of the trailer where their design was taking shape. "That's all you girls. I'm on the construction team."

The belt slid from his hips to his feet, the hammer knocking against the wood trailer floor with a thud.

"Aww," Nelda said, "Look Whitney, the macho man can't even keep his belt up."

14

COMING CLEAN REDUX

Wednesday Morning, November 20th
Tech Success, Inc.
Denver, Colorado

L acie took off the reading glasses she wore when her eyes were too tired for her contacts. She tried to look at the time on her computer screen, but realizing she couldn't see it, she slid them back on again. 4:32 AM. She took the glasses back off and rubbed her eyes, then stood and stretched out the kinks in her back.

"An hour and a half in," she said aloud in the empty cavern of cubicles. *I've made some progress. A plan is taking shape. I just hope management isn't so blindsided by my screwup they miss the bigger picture.* She sat back down and pulled her usual reports and began to work those. She wanted her normal workload out of the way when she hit management with her admission and her resulting center sponsorship plan.

. . .

LACIE LOOKED around the small conference room table. Other than Connie from HR, the management group present was made up of straight, white males. She sucked in a deep breath and plunged ahead.

"Good morning, Connie, gentlemen." She dipped her head to acknowledge first the head of HR and then the three men arrayed around the table. "I apologize for any calendar switching that happened for any of you in advance, and I promise not to take up a lot of your time. I only need about a half hour of your time this morning."

She saw Jim, the Vice President of the IT group and her boss, check his watch. *He's retiring after the first of the year. What's his hurry?*

Movement outside the corner room with both sidewalls of glass caught her eye. Heaven was walking past in the hallway carrying an armload of files. She only had eyes for Lacie. Looking away, she continued, "I've invited Connie up here for a very specific reason. This past summer, I got into some legal trouble one evening after a couple of poor decisions."

Connie leaned forward in her chair, toward her. Jim, in contrast, sat back, crossed his arms over his chest and stared at her unblinkingly. She couldn't read his expression.

"I was eventually charged with a minor misdemeanor and given no jail time or probation, just community service." She paused and looked at Connie. "It should not affect my background check or status with the company in any way, according to the handbook, but I'll do what I need to do to give all reassurances to HR and," she looked around the table, "to all of you."

Jim glowered at her. "Why are we just hearing this?

She swallowed hard and tried to take her lumps. "No excuses. I was scared of what might happen with... with the potential promotion when you leave. I... I'm the most senior of the senior business analysts and one of only three, that I'm aware of, who are interested in the position."

"That decision hasn't been made," Damon Tollison, the CTO, said.

"I appreciate that. I... " she spied Heaven walking back by and turned away, trying to focus anywhere but on the area beyond the glass. "I hope to convince all of you that I'm still a worthy candidate."

"You are correct, a minor misdemeanor is not disqualifying for employment with Tech Success," Connie offered. "You do, I'm sure, have documentation?"

Lacie nodded. "And I'll submit to a full background and records check, at my own expense."

"That would be advisable, Ms. Lindly," Jim said, being more formal with her than he'd ever been. "I take it by you bringing this up now has something to do with your 'special project?' he said, as he made air quotes.

She did her best to school her features and keep a professional demeanor. "That's correct. My project, one I hope the company agrees to back, involves the Sun Valley Community Recreation Center where I'm doing my community service."

"Sun Valley?" Tollison's tone was skeptical.

Apparently, Heaven only got to the department head... a break for me. "Yes, sir."

"Damon, please Lacie."

"Yes, Damon. Sun Valley, over near Mile High and all the recreational development that's gone on in that area."

Jim scoffed. "I wasn't aware there was any."

Connie came to her rescue. "Gentlemen, if I may before I take my leave, there's quite a bit that's going on over there. A whole revitalization of the area. My husband is with one of the developers. But I'm sure Lacie's done her homework. I'll leave her to it." She stood.

"Thank you," Lacie said, trying to keep the relief out of her voice. "I'll be down as soon as I'm finished here to take care of whatever you need."

Connie gave her a nod, gathered her unused notepad, and left the conference room.

Lacie took a deep breath and assumed her usual business analyst tone. "Gentlemen, I'm proposing that we, as 'Tech Success' invest in the success of the Sun Valley community by putting our money where our mouth is. Under what I'm about to propose, we'll reap benefits far beyond what we spend. We're all about success, after all, and Sun Valley is a neighborhood that could use a lot more of it. Short term, we should help them meet their year-end needs. Longer term, I propose we assist by putting a computer lab and learning programs in place in the community. We invest in free Wi-Fi—"

Heaven started past the room again. Lacie stepped toward the door and waved her in. *Two can play this game.*

The other woman looked away at first, but then turned and, head held high, entered the room. "Did you need something, Lacie?"

"I did. I wanted to thank you for giving Jim a heads up on my project and invite you to assist. Regardless of what's decided here today, I still need a lot of hands."

She looked around the room at the three men staring back at her. "Um, yeah sure. Of course. Whatever you need."

"Great! Thanks so much."

Heaven started to leave. Lacie held up a hand. "You're welcome to stay. I was just getting to the immediate needs."

"Sorry. I... I've got things I need to get to."

She feigned indifference, saying, "Suit yourself. We'll talk more later," then paused a few beats while Heaven left, pulling the door closed behind her. *That's probably going to bite me in the ass, but it was so worth it.*

LACIE GOT to the center several minutes later than usual. She took the still open front spot, figuring that since it was Wednesday, Sophia would have taken the bus over from campus.

Inside, she found Will in the area off the gym floor where tables were usually set up, but Sophia was nowhere in sight. Will was moving about frantically, dragging tables away from the walls where they'd been pushed. He sketched a wave at her as he explained, "Had a floor cleaning crew in here today. They come every few weeks or so. Usually, Sophia helps me do this."

Lacie moved to the other end of the table he was pulling, picked it up, and helped him move it into position. "She's not here then, I take it?"

"Not yet." His voice gave away his concern.

"That's odd, right?"

He nodded. "Might be a late bus or something. Usually though, if anything weird is happening, she calls or texts."

"That's too bad. I have a lot to tell her... both of you. Good news, that—"

The main door swung open and boisterous voices filtered through as the children began arriving from school. "Sorry," Will said. "It's going to have to wait."

They finished moving the tables, then Lacie shooed Will toward the kitchenette while she got everyone out of their outer garments and settled in with their schoolwork.

"Let's get going, kids," she told them. "Remember, my friend Ted is coming today and he's going to help us work with the lights for our float." *Our float. I like the sound of that. Weird Sofia isn't here, though. She knew he was coming today.* She thought about pulling out her phone and texting her, but she decided against it, figuring Will probably already had.

. . .

SOFIA CAME IN WITH BRITTNEY, both all apologetic, about ten minutes after the children arrived. Lacie was confused. "I thought you had a later class on Wednesday, Britt?"

"Normally yes. My professor was only holding office hours today since we have the mid-term on Monday, before the Thanksgiving break. Sophia just waited around for me while I met with him."

"Well, I'm glad you're both here. I have some great news from my company to share with you and Will when we all have a minute." She said it to both women, but she only had eyes for Sophia.

Sophia cracked a sliver of a smile, filling Lacie's heart.

Her euphoria wasn't long lived. Moments later, when Will peeked out of the little kitchenette and called the kids in to pick up their snacks, Ted arrived, trailed by Heaven. Lacie swallowed hard. *I wasn't expecting her. I thought bringing her in this morning would have scared her off.* She glanced over at Sophia. The younger woman was standing stock still, staring at Heaven.

Britt looked between the two of them. "Does someone want to tell me what's going on?"

Heaven answered before anyone else could. "Lacie invited me to help with the project. Well, she basically called me out in front of management, so here I am, and I want an explanation."

"So do I," Sofia managed.

Lacie dipped her head and acknowledged the two newcomers. She directed her attention primarily to Ted as she said, "Ted, Heaven, you two have met Sophia. This is Brittney."

"Britt is fine," Brittney said as she extended her hand first to Heaven and then to Ted, when the thirty-something-year-old woman didn't bother to take it.

Ted's discomfort showed as he dug at the collar of his button down with his left hand while he shook Britt's offered hand with his right. "Nice... nice to meet you."

Trying to keep it light, Lacie extended an arm toward the kitchen where Will was walking out. "That's Will, the center director and our resident float construction expert."

"Float?" Heaven questioned.

"Yes. That's the project." *Currently, anyway,* Lacie thought. "We're helping the center with their holiday parade float." *Among other things.*

Hand on her hip, Heaven raised an eyebrow, "All of this sneaking around, for a *float*?" Her stance and tone had the attention of most of the older kids, who looked on quietly as they munched their snacks, something unusual for the typically boisterous group.

"Sneaking around?" Will asked as he approached the group.

"No sneaking around," Lacie said. "You already know what's going on and so does Sofia." She motioned Ted forward. "Will, this is Ted. Why don't you take him and show him the construction that's been done so far and the lights we have, while I bring Heaven up to speed?"

LACIE DIRECTED Heaven toward the front door, as far away from the rest of the people in the main area of the rec center as possible, but still within eyesight of everything else that was happening. Britt had been about to follow them, but she watched Sophia pull her in the opposite direction when most of the children jumped up, leaving their snacks behind, and followed Will and Ted over to the growing float.

"What's going on Lacie?" Heaven all but hissed at her.

"Exactly what you see. We're building a parade float for the center to put in the holiday parade."

"Simple as that, huh?"

No. "Yes, it's that simple."

Both hands on her hips, Heaven leaned in, bringing her face

within inches of Lacie's. "I. Don't. Buy. It," she said, her voice rising with each word. "What aren't you telling me?"

Lacie saw Will and Ted looking their way. She took Heaven's arm and turned her so her back was to the two men, then dropped it. "Look, it's a long story—"

"I've got all evening."

Lacie held up a hand to stay her as she stifled a yawn with the back of her other hand. "And I don't. I'm exhausted. I've got to get these guys going and get out of here, get some rest so I can do it all again tomorrow. The gist is this, this center is in dire straits. They've lost funding. They serve a needy, deserving community and they don't deserve to be closed. A lot of the kids have nowhere else to go but the streets after school if they get turned out of here."

"What's that got to do with us... with the company? Because, when I talked to Jim yesterday, it didn't seem like he knew a damn thing."

Lacie mentally bit her tongue. *Don't lash out. Don't lash out.* "The company is helping with some year-end stuff I took a little higher than Jim because it was last minute." *Not really a lie... just timing.*

"Then, what was the meeting this morning all about?"

"That was higher level planning, going forward." *Okay,* she told herself, *Not a complete lie, I just hope they bite on my ideas.*

WHILE TED CLIMBED up on the float trailer with a tape measure, Will said to Sophia and Britt, "That looks like a whole lot of drama over there." He tipped his head toward the two women by the front door.

"That woman, um, she works with Lacie and Ted. I met her the other day. She's... "

When she trailed off, Will said, "We just don't need that right now, so maybe we should cut our losses with Lacie."

"Can we talk for a minute?" She tipped her head, imploring Will to step away with her.

"Okay, I admit," she whispered, "Lacie can be a handful, but she's had some great ideas and she really does seem to want to help."

"You don't know why she's really here. She doesn't have a choice but to—"

Sofia interrupted him. "I do know why. She told me everything. She says she has news and I have an idea what it might be. Whatever it is, I'm sure it's going to be something good for the center. Let's not get too far ahead of ourselves; give her a chance."

"WHAT ABOUT HER?" Heaven asked. She jabbed her thumb over her shoulder in the direction of the float. "Sophia?"

"She works here. I actually work for her and for Will when I'm here."

"It's a lot more than that."

"No, it really isn't."

"You dumped me for her."

"Again, no. She and I are not involved." *Not for a lack of interest on my part.* "And, frankly, we both realize you and I are never going to work as a couple. I don't have the time for a relationship right now with anyone and we're very different people."

"Opposites attract."

Lacie groaned. "We're so opposite, we want completely different things. It won't work. You want a whole lifestyle that doesn't interest me in the least."

Heaven half turned and waved an arm about, "And this does?"

"I don't know and I'm too tired to think about it right now." *I was in the office at 3:00 AM because of you.* "I know that I want to be fulfilled by what I do; satisfied."

"You're not going to be paid what you're worth in a dump like this!"

Lacie bristled. "Money is the last thing on my mind right now."

Heaven rolled her eyes.

"I need to get over there and help them out. Are you helping or not?"

Heaven didn't hesitate, "That'd be a hard no." She pushed past Lacie and went outside.

Lacie didn't follow. She walked over to Sophia and Britt now standing side by side watching Ted as he explained what he needed to Will.

She came up behind them and put a hand on a shoulder of each. "Sorry about that. I don't think she'll be back."

As both women turned toward her, she dropped her hands, but she regretted it as another yawn came over her in a wave.

"Are you all right?" Brittney asked her.

"Sorry." She stifled a second yawn. "I'm so sorry. I went in really early this morning to put some stuff together for my company and now I'm just totally whipped."

"You should go home," Sophia said.

Will jumped down off the float and joined their group. "Everything okay?" His tone told Lacie he was asking about more than just her physical state.

She gave him a nod. "We're good. It's all good, and I have a lot to share with you, but it will have to wait. Again, I'm so sorry. I was at work just before 3:00 AM this morning, and I feel like I'm about to drop."

"Can I drive you home?" Will offered.

She waved him off. "It's not that far. Can you all be here, say around 2:00 tomorrow, so we can talk?"

"Me too?" Brittney asked.

"Yes, if you can."

Britt gave her a quick nod. "I'll split my day at the ranch and make it work."

Lacie sketched a wave goodbye to the group as she headed for the coat rack, then remembered something. Calling over her shoulder, she told the three of them, "And keep Saturday night open too, if you can. You're all invited to a party at The Lake House at Cherry Creek, that I'm sure you'll want to go to. Business casual."

HER PHONE BUZZED WITH A TEXT. She almost didn't pick it up.

SOFIA: Did you make it home okay?

Lacie: Yes

Lacie: Thank you. I appreciate your concern.

Sofia: See you tomorrow

Lacie: Yes. I'll be there at 2:00 with bells on.

Sofia: LOL

Sofia: Get some rest

Lacie: Headed to bed now. Goodnight.

Sofia: Sweet dreams

LACIE SMILED as she plugged her phone into the charger and climbed into bed.

15

PLANNING COMMITTEE

Thursday, November 21st
Sun Valley Community Recreation Center
Denver, Colorado

Sofia drummed her fingers on the high-top table. Will didn't seem to notice her nervousness as he tapped out an email on his phone, but Brittney reached out and stilled her hand as she gave her a look.

Sofia raised an eyebrow at her friend. "Am I annoying you?"

"Just wondering what you're so nervous about."

"I'm not nervous," she denied as she twisted a finger through a long lock of hair.

Lacie strolled in at 1:58 and set a carrier with four takeout cups down on the high table. She started talking as she took off her coat. "It's not coffee, it's hot chocolate." She laughed as Brittney reached right out for a cup.

"Don't mind if I do. Thanks, Lacie!"

"I'm glad you're all here and ready to go. I have a lot I want to tell you before the kids get here." She hung her coat on the second hook down next to Sofia's, then glanced again at Britt, taking in the fact that she still had her outwear on. "Not sticking around?"

"I have to go back to work at the ranch. A lot going on today."

"I'm so sorry," Lacie began, but Britt waved her off.

"It's okay. I wanted to be here for this and my boss, this one's dad," she said as she tapped elbows with Sofia, "is very understanding."

"Well, I'll get right to it, then. In the interest of full disclosure, Brittney, I'm here in the first place doing community service I was ordered to do by Judge Hildalgo, whom I'm assuming you're familiar with?"

Brittney answered with raised eyebrows, but then she refocused on blowing into the opening in her cup to cool the liquid enough to take a taste.

"It's a long story, but the gist is I'm doing this time for a minor misdemeanor. Sofia can tell you all about it later."

She tipped her head toward the younger woman. "It's fine to tell her. It's all out in the open."

She took a seat and pulled the last cup out of the carrier. "Anyway, I disclosed everything to my company yesterday morning, something I'm ashamed to admit, I hadn't done."

Sophia jumped in, "Did... did everything go okay?"

"Better than I expected. Let's put it that way. The, uh, jury is still out on some things." She shrugged. For Britt's benefit, she added, "Because they didn't know why I was here... or really, that I was here, they didn't know about Ted helping or any of that."

Will sat back. "Oh. I didn't realize that. That's a problem, then, isn't it?"

She shook her head. "Not anymore. Ted, bless him, would have helped anyway because, well, that's Ted. Now though, we have full blessing to use company assets to assist with the float and even to help with the parade in any other way we might need."

"You're sure?" Will asked.

Lacie held up three fingers. "Scout's honor. And, the beauty part is, I can return to my normal work hours instead of going in two or three hours early. They're fully supporting my being here and... er... doing my time, so to speak."

Sofia couldn't help herself. "Wow! I didn't see that coming."

"That makes two of us," Lacie said. "I still have to get my usual workload done, but it's a lot slower this time of year, so it shouldn't be a problem. Here's the thing, and it wasn't decided yesterday, per se, but I found out this morning; short term, they're going to pay for and support the center in any way you need, including financing what you need for the holiday party." She paused as eyes grew wide around the table and the other three leaned in.

"You're kidding?" Will asked.

"Wow," was all Sofia could manage for a moment.

Britt was the first one to come to her senses. "What all does that include, *exactly*?"

"It means, let's plan a party and figure out who all is coming. Food, decorations, gifts, everything."

Will slapped the table. "I'm with Sofia. Wow! Is there a spending limit?"

"They're willing to go to ten grand, but if we need more—" She trailed off when she took note of the expressions around the table.

"That's more than twice what we usually spend," Will said. "I think we'll be okay."

"Um, yeah," Britt added.

"Good. Let's circle back to talking about the party in a minute. I did want to tell you, and I hope I wasn't overstepping, but I actually proposed a much longer-term relationship with the center to them."

Will spoke first, "Like what?"

"Upgrades to this building, for starters, and possibly some additional development down the road after a study. That could include a computer lab and Wi-Fi and community training, because that's what you really do here. I know some of that isn't necessarily in keeping with a recreation theme, but I look at this place more as a community service center than a rec center."

"And," Will said, "Denver is getting ready to reopen the Rude Center a few blocks from here that they just remodeled. We change, or we die."

There were nods around the table.

Lacie took a deep breath. "That part's not a done deal, so I don't want you to get your hopes too high, but I'm going to do everything in my power to make it happen. The management wants a lot more information. They've agreed that I can spend some of my work time doing more analysis on site, after the first of the year, and they'll back that with judge Hildalgo. They won't make a firm commitment until they have more data about what the building and the property can support and how much community utilization it will get."

"Fair enough," Will said. "Fair enough. And, of course, whatever you need from me, is yours."

"That reminds me, if you remember, I mentioned as I was crawling out of here yesterday afternoon, about keeping Saturday evening open?"

When the other three nodded, she told them, "You're all invited to our company holiday party - yes, we have it early. I'll introduce you around to all the key players. You can, if you're up for it, help me to convince them. And, there'll be lots of food, open bar, the whole deal. It's a tech bunch though, so don't expect things to get too crazy."

"Me too?" Brittney asked.

"Yes, you too, and bring your fiancé." She looked at Will. "You wear a wedding band, so I assume you're married. Bring your spouse."

"I may just do that," Will said. "She loves that sort of thing and just going out and doing something in general, to be honest. She'll be here a lot as we gear up for the Christmas party."

"I can't wait to meet her." She turned toward Sofia, "You can certainly bring someone too, if you like."

Brittney jumped in with, "Are you taking a date, Lacie?"

Sofia blanched at the question. She wanted to kick Britt under the table, but in their close quarters she was afraid she might hit Will or Lacie instead.

"Um, that would be a no," Lacie responded.

Sofia felt relief wash over her. "It'll just be me alone as well, I guess." She did her best to hide her smile when Lacie said, 'Good,' before moving on.

"It starts at 7:00 at the Lake House at Cherry Creek, if I didn't mention that yesterday, and I'm here to tell you that in my experience, it will be over by 10:00, so get all your glad handing, meeting, and greeting done by 9:00 or so. Party animals these guys are not."

"You're sure they won't mind us being there?" Sofia asked.

Lacie turned toward her. "People from other ventures and other organizations 'T.S.' supports will be there too. If we start working with the center long term - and I'm sure we will - you'll be invited back annually." She looked at her watch, then clapped her hands together. "We have about ten minutes before we have to start preparing for the kids." She took a swig of her cooling cocoa and then said, "Let's talk about the center's party."

"It's more about the kids than anything," Will said, "but there's always been something included for their caregivers too."

Sofia added, "And for other children, too. Sometimes there

are other kids in their lives - older and younger - that don't necessarily come to us on a daily basis who come to the party."

"Okay." Lacie blew out a breath. "How do you usually handle that from a gift perspective?"

Will was the first to answer. "We usually have an idea how many are coming, and the ages and Santa has some age-appropriate gifts laid aside."

"They're just happy to be here, be safe, eat and get a little something," Britt said.

"Exactly," Sofia added. "It's a night for them, once a year. We'll send out reminders about it after the first of December and start feeling the kids out about who's coming."

"How does the shopping work?"

"Britt and me," Sophia pointed between them, "my dad, some other volunteers... Mrs. Hildalgo."

"So, you need the money by when, or how does that all work?"

"You and I can work that out later," Will said. "We only have a few minutes or so before it's business as usual around here."

"Yes," Sofia said, "Let's talk about the entertainment."

Lacie answered, "I still think we do a show with the regular kids, and I had another idea about that. Clevon wants to do stand-up, right? What if we give him a few minutes, but we also let him MC, put his usual antics to use?"

Will chuckled. "That could be very cute."

"Maybe," Sofia said, but she didn't feel so sure. "He'd have to keep it clean. All of it."

Britt piped up, "I love it and I think we have more than enough time to work with Clevon and the other older kids like Whitney and Nelda, to pull it off."

16

GIRL FIGHT!

The kids began arriving while Lacie was in the break room, disposing of their cocoa cups. *That all went over pretty well.* She was smiling to herself and in a good mood as she started to walk out of the kitchenette. The sounds of an argument stopped her cold.

She watched as Nelda and Whitney went head-to-head in an argument over something she'd come into the middle of. One look at Clevon's face as he tried to get between them and say something told her all she needed to know. She rushed toward them, but she wasn't the only one. Will and Sofia converged on the whole group of kids, too. Sofia started directing the little ones away as Will put his body squarely between the two young women.

"If you're going to get physical," he cautioned them, "you're going to have to get through me."

Clevon tried to step forward, but Will told him, "Back off. I've got this." He looked from one teen girl to the other. "Let's all calm down. Both of you, take a couple of steps back, give each other some breathing room."

The girls hesitated at first, but with the much larger Will

continuing to glower at them, they gave in and did as they were told.

Lacie motioned Clevon to her. When the boy moved in her direction, she guided him to the kitchenette, saying, "Let's talk in here."

He followed, skulking behind her.

She didn't mince word with him. "I know you know what that was all about. They're arguing over you, aren't they?"

He gave her a half shrug. "I dunno. I guess so. I didn't start nothin' between them."

"I'm not blaming you." She met his eyes, "But I do want to ask you, do you have feelings for either of them?" *As if I don't really know the answer.*

"Me and Whitney have been going out a little bit... a couple of times."

Okay, not the answer I was expecting.

"And Nelda?"

He shook his head. "She's my neighbor, two doors down. I've been knowing her for forever."

"Ever go out with her?"

"No, no. She's too young... just turned 13 last month, I think, or the month before. And, anyway, she's a year behind me in school. We just... we hang out sometimes. My gramma and hers are friends." He trailed off with that statement and let out a small sigh.

Something else is wrong. "What are you worried about?" When he didn't answer, she prodded him again. "What's really on your mind?"

"Nothin.' I'm fine."

"It's not nothing if it's bothering you. You've got two beautiful young women fighting over you, to state the obvious, and you're in here all moon-faced instead of out there strutting around like a banty rooster."

"My gramma says that... that banty rooster thing."

"Did she grow up on a farm like I did?"

He shrugged again.

"Anyway," Lacie said, "back to the subject; what's up?"

Clevon gave in. "DeMarco wasn't in school today. I think him and his mom may have been evicted after all. I mean, we seem like we fight and all, but we're friends. I don't want him to have to move."

Her heart sank. *Buck up. Sofia tried to tell you.* "Tell you what, I'll talk to Will, see if he can go around and check on him, see if there's anything we can do to help them, okay?"

He gave her a small nod, but then said, "It might be better if Sofia went. DeMarco has a hard time with men. They've never been there for him."

"Even Will?"

"I dunno. I just know what I've seen hanging around with him."

"Let us work on that, okay?" When he nodded again, she told him, "Now, let's get it together because you have a young woman out there wondering what's going on and you have a lot of work to do."

"Say what?"

"You heard me; work." She drew the last word out. "We're doing a show at the holiday party and, not only are you going to do your stand-up, but you're also going to be the MC."

"MC? What's that?"

She clapped him on the back. "You have so much to learn!"

IN THE MULTIPURPOSE ROOM, the younger kids were at the tables pulling out homework, and Sofia had joined Will and the girls. Lacie led Clevon toward their group.

Nelda spoke up. "I'm sorry, Clevon. I didn't mean to start anything with you."

Lacie raised her eyebrows at Sofia in a look only she could see, but she stayed mum.

"It's okay," he said. "I'm sorry too. I like you, but like a sister. We've always hung together, and—"

"Don't worry about it," Nelda said. "We're good."

"Sure?" He tilted his head, giving her a look.

"I'm sure."

Lacie looked at Clevon and then at Whitney. "I won't try and pretend to be a parent to either of you or anything of the sort here. I just want you two to take it slow and be very, very careful."

Whitney shot Clevon a look that Sofia caught. She jumped in, saying, "We can all see it, guys. We're not blind and dumb, here."

"My grandmother would kill me, if I... I... you know," Whitney said, dropping her head, not meeting anyone's eyes.

"Good," Will said. He turned to Clevon. "And I'll kill you. Your gramma may not be able to catch you, but I can."

Clevon swallowed hard. "Yes, sir."

Will clapped his hands together as he often did. "Now that, that's settled, we need to talk with you three about something coming up really quickly and then you all need to get on your homework. Ted is coming back tonight and we're going to finish rigging the lights."

"What else do you want to talk to us about?" Nelda asked.

Lacie moved away to supervise the homework for the younger kids, while Will and Sofia sketched out the holiday show idea for the three teens.

∾

Sofia

WHEN THEY PREPARED THE SNACKS, Lacie told Sofia about DeMarco.

With Will's blessing and multiple cautions, after closing and clean-up, the two women went in Lacie's Outback over to the public housing development where many of the center children lived.

At DeMarco's door, Sofia noticed staples that were holding the corner of a piece of paper that had been torn off. She was about to point it out to Lacie when DeMarco's mother answered their knock, surprising her.

"Hi Ms. Chase. I wasn't sure you'd be here."

"We got another day."

"I meant, I thought you'd probably be at work."

"That's why we only got one more day here. My hours got cut. I couldn't meet my part of the rent over what Section Eight pays."

"Can we come in, Ms. Chase? It's pretty cold tonight," Sofia asked.

"I suppose. Don't mind the mess. We're trying to pack." She held the door wide and stepped back so they could pass.

"This is Lacie," Sofia said by way of introduction. She looked around at the room. It was disarrayed in a lived-in sort of way. DeMarco sat on a broken-down sofa, the only seating in the room, staring at the two of them. There were a couple of boxes with items in them stacked by the door, the only evidence any packing had been going on.

"They didn't give you much notice, I take it?" Lacie asked.

"Thirty days. What they have to give. I've been looking for something else. Ain't had no luck."

Sofia squeezed her eyes shut for just a moment. "Do you have somewhere to go?" *Because they'll yank you out of here tomorrow and that door will be padlocked whether your stuff is out or not.*

"We can probably stay with my sister across town for a bit, till I can find something."

"What about your hours?" Lacie asked.

"There is that. Gotta find another part-time job on the bus line too. Don't want to give up the one I got though. It's a good job. Things are just slow right now."

Lacie asked, "Where's that?"

"Chicken place, over by the stadium. Wish the Broncos played all their games at home; then I'd get my hours."

"DeMarco is going to have to change schools if you move across town," Sofia said. "Wouldn't you like to keep him in the same school for the rest of the school year?" Sofia asked.

DeMarco stood. "I want to stay in this school, Mama."

She waved her son back down. "Boy, if I could figure this out, you know you would. At least through Christmas, I would keep you there."

"I'm going to be really forward here," Lacie said. "How much do you need to get back to even here?"

"Say what?"

"How far behind are you?"

The other woman shrugged. "Two months on my part of the rent. About $580.00."

"And," Sofia said more to Lacie than to the woman she only knew as Ms. Chase, "rent is probably due on the first. So, that's another $290 in ten days, if they even agree to let her pay it and stay."

Lacie was taken aback. "Why wouldn't they let her stay, if she paid the money?"

"I ain't got the money, regardless."

Sofia glanced over at DeMarco, then said softly, "Once an eviction is in motion, it's hard to reverse."

"But we could try, right?" Lacie asked.

"Yeah. I guess," Sofia said, "But I don't have access to that kind of money."

"Let me handle that."

Sofia eyed Lacie, but before she could say anything to her, DeMarco's mother jumped in. "I ain't taking no charity. I work for what I have, when and where I can."

"It wouldn't be charity, I promise. I'm talking about a loan with a job to back it up, probably part time to start and pretty close to here. Certainly, on the bus line. I can make some calls in the morning and get it all set up. How much time do we have with this Section Eight stuff?"

"We gotta be out by 4:00 tomorrow afternoon."

"Plenty of time," Lacie said with as much confidence as she could muster. "How do you feel about working on a cleaning crew?"

"Ain't nothing I haven't done before."

"WHAT DO you have up your sleeve?" Sophia asked once they were back in Lacie's car.

"Ball Arena."

"The basketball arena?"

"And hockey, concerts, monster trucks, and whatever else they can schedule in there. The company contracted to clean it also cleans our building. I know a few people in charge there pretty well. It's on the bus line, and they're always advertising for arena cleaning crew help because the schedule is so varied. It sounds like it might work perfect for her if she can find help with DeMarco."

"You just keep right on surprising me."

"Good." Lacie smiled. "Good."

"Now, I know that rent money is probably coming out of your pocket, so how are you setting up this so-called loan?"

"I haven't figured that part out yet."

BACK AT THE CENTER, Lacie pulled up alongside Sofia's car and winced. The compact had been broken into; the driver's side window smashed in.

Sofia jumped out of the Outback to check out the damage while Lacie parked. She stood there, alongside the car in the street, rubbing her arms, when Lacie walked up beside her.

Lacie looked inside and took in the wires hanging out of the steering column. "Looks like they tried to hot wire it. I didn't think you could still do that on cars that were made in this century."

She turned back to Sofia when the younger woman sobbed and instinctively embraced her.

"This has never happened before," Sophia sobbed. "I've always been so careful, never left anything valuable in it."

"It's okay," Lacie said, pulling back a little and wiping a tear from Sophia's face. "It's going to be okay."

Sophia took a few shallow breaths and dabbed at her own tears.

Lacie backed off a half step. "We need to call the police and a tow."

"Okay, on the police. No tow. I'll... I'll call Frank. He'll come and get it... tonight, I hope."

"Do you have insurance, Sofia?"

"Liability. It's twelve years old." Another tear fell.

Lacie hugged her again. "We'll figure it out."

Sofia threw her head back. "Guess I'm going to be working for that cleaning company too."

"No," Lacie said. "Not a chance. Don't worry about it, okay? Talk to Frank, first. He may have an idea how to help you."

"I'M GOING to drop the car at the garage before I head home," Frank said. "You're welcome to ride along, but it will be a bit."

Lacie volunteered, "I can run you home."

"You're both too nice, but Lacie, it's out of your way."

"We've been over this. It's not that far, another ten minutes... or so."

Frank said, "It's going to be an hour or more for me. I'm going to leave a message for Central Salvage too, before I get back on the road. If they have a window that will fit, I'll pick it up on my rounds tomorrow. Our glass guy can probably have you back on the road tomorrow evening."

"How much is that going to cost me?"

Frank ticked off two fingers. "About ten bucks for the window, and around fifty bucks for the install, give or take. It shouldn't take him long, as long as central has one."

"Fingers crossed," Lacie said.

"IT'S AFTER 6:30," Lacie said. She pointed at the Torchy's Tacos location. "Do you mind? My treat."

"Are you sure?"

"Of course." She turned into the parking lot.

"I could eat."

"They don't have a drive through, though."

"Oh. You probably want to get home... "

"I was thinking about you, Sofia."

"Tacos are fine. Great even. I love their food, but I don't get it very often."

"I do too and neither do I."

"Probably not for the same reasons," Sofia said.

"Try me."

"I can't afford it. Poor college student."

"And I try not to splurge too often. I'm careful with my money," she said as she undid her seatbelt and started to get out of the car.

Sofia's answer stayed her. "You could have fooled me. Lights for the center, rent for Ms. Chase... "

"Who will be paying me back," Lacie bantered back.

"Says you."

"She will. Over time. A long time. And, for the record," she said as she held the door open for the younger woman, "those are things I wanted to do and can afford to. I've been saving and putting back for a long time. It's always been just me and I'm going to be the only one taking care of me in my old age."

"I doubt you'll be all alone in your old age."

"Is that an offer?"

Sophia colored. "That's... that's not what I meant. I meant, you're getting up there now, but you're—"

Stopping just outside the restaurant, Lacie threw a hand to her hip, "I beg your pardon!"

"This is coming out all wrong." Sophia opened the door herself and stepped inside, holding it open behind her for Lacie.

A smiling server saved her further embarrassment. "Two? Right this way."

17

A CORPORATE AFFAIR

Saturday Night, November 23rd
Tech Success, Inc. Pre-holiday Event
Denver, Colorado

S ofia cruised along slowly, looking at the building numbers. When she found the one Lacie gave her for her townhouse condo, she parked her car in the front, being sure not to block the short driveway in front of the garage, then checked her hair in the rear-view mirror.

She stepped out and gave the door a firm close after being sure to push the lock button. The new to her replacement window was the cleanest of all of her windows she realized as she checked her reflection and smoothed her sweater down over the top of her skirt. *Hope I look okay.*

She pulled her unbuttoned, calf length coat tight around her when she shivered against the night air as she walked up the short walkway Lacie's door.

Lacie answered quickly, saying, "I saw you out the front window. You look amazing."

Sophia's blush was hidden by the wind burn to her cheeks from a day spent working with the horses at the ranch. She took in Lacie in her black slacks and open collar burgundy blouse that matched the main color in her own plaid wool skirt. *She looks so good, no matter what she wears.* She couldn't trust herself to voice the thought without stammering. Instead, she looked around, taking in the woodwork all around her and the gleaming stainless-steel appliances visible in the open kitchen. "You have a really nice, um, apartment. Townhouse, I guess. Very nice."

"Townhouse. Well, actually it's a condo. I own it. It's nice because I don't have a payment other than my taxes and my condo fees, and they take care of all the maintenance stuff."

"I can only dream of ever having a place like this even when I have my master's."

Lacie shrugged the thought off. "It has its drawbacks too, like neighbors for one, and no real private outdoor area unless you count my second-floor balcony, but it works for my life right now. Would you like to see the rest?"

"Like the bedrooms?" *Now, what made me say that?*

"Bedroom, singular, but yes. I set the second one up as a small home office or a den, if you prefer to call it that." She gave Sofia her megawatt grin.

"Sure... I guess that would be okay." Her neck felt hot.

"No pressure."

"I... it's fine. Lead the way."

"No, after you." Lacie placed a hand at the small of her back and guided her across the living area into a short hallway. She pushed open a door on the left. "Powder room."

The door on the right was open. She turned her slightly that way and pointed inside. "The office. It comes with a small bathroom since it's supposed to be a bedroom, and as you can see, it has a window that looks out of the end of this building at the next building over. Great view, that."

"I bet." She could feel every nerve ending in her back where Lacie's hand touched as she guided her forward toward the stairs. When they reached the top where they opened out, Sofia swallowed hard, glad Lacie couldn't see her face as she got her first view of the massive master bedroom that took up most of the second floor.

A high four-poster bed made up with silk sheets and a heavy comforter dominated the center of the room. It faced the same sidewall the office was on, but instead of a window, there was a gas fireplace that rose from the floor up and a flat screen TV hanging on the wall above the wood mantle.

The wall opposite the entry into the room was mostly glass. The curtains were partially open, revealing French doors out to the balcony Lacie had mentioned.

Lacie attempted to usher her around the bed.

"This is very lovely... but I never pictured you as a four-poster bed kind of person."

"What kind of bed did you picture me with?" She quirked an eyebrow, then grinned at Sofia's mortified expression.

"I think I've said... we've seen enough."

Lacie didn't let her off the hook. "Oh, but you have to see the bathroom. It's what sold the place for me." She gently propelled her forward toward the double doorway on the opposite side of the bed.

Sofia stepped into the largest, most luxurious bathroom she had ever seen. When she entered, she caught the familiar scent of the cologne Lacie typically wore. She breathed in deep, without realizing what she was doing.

On the left wall, a doorway led into a walk-in closet. Beyond that was a sink and vanity with lights surrounding it. A masculine looking cologne bottle sat on the counter, confirming the source of the scent. There was a commode in its own little half-wall stall, and on the back wall, a massive sunken tub. The right wall had a stone and glass shower stall with a rain head shower. "Unreal. Absolutely unreal. I would never leave that tub... or that shower, either one."

"I admit, it's tough."

She turned into Lacie's hand, then suppressed a shiver when she felt the heat of the older woman's breath on her face. "It's about a quarter to seven. We should probably go," she managed to squeak out.

"Yeah," Lacie said without taking her eyes off Sophia's face. "Tech geeks are never late."

"Brittney and Frank won't be either," Sofia said as she took a step back. "She's pretty excited."

"I'm surprised you didn't come with them, and you were willing to meet up with me."

"They don't get to spend much time together these days. He's working extra hours to pay for the wedding while she tries to get school finished."

"What she's doing after school?"

"Funny you asked. We were just talking about that." *And about you helping her meet some people.* "She's got a job in retail management lined up."

Lacie pulled a face.

"Exactly," Sofia said. "She'll have a management degree with a heavy background in marketing. She'd really like to do more with that than merchandizing and... " She waved a hand in the air. "You know, working evenings, overnight, weekends, holidays, that sort of thing."

"She's going to meet some people tonight that might be willing to help her find something more suitable. I'll try to introduce her around to some of them. The rest though is up to her."

"Lacie, that's great. Really great of you. Thank you."

Brushing off the gratitude, Lacie looked at her watch and said, "You were right. We really should get going."

AS THEY APPROACHED THE VENUE, Sofia unclasped her hands from her lap and wiped her sweaty palms against her coat.

"Nervous?"

"A little. I've never been to a high-class sort of party like this before."

Lacie snorted. "Sweetie, I promise you, it's not high class. They're just regular people with a geeky side, yours truly included."

Sofia heard very little after the word, 'sweetie,' which she knew in the back of her mind Lacie was using informally, not as a term of endearment. *Or is she?* "I know. I just struggle a little when I'm out of my comfort zone. I'll work through it." *For the party anyway. I'm not so sure about why I feel so drawn to you and how to deal with that.*

She asked the question that had been nagging at her. "What about Heaven?"

"She'll be here, but don't you worry about her. She'll have bigger fish to fry tonight."

She was relieved when they arrived and found Brittney and Frank getting out of Frank's pickup. She admired the fact that he'd washed it for the occasion.

"Judging by the parking lot," Britt said, "this shindig is already in full swing."

Lacie chuckled. "Full swing, you'll see is a relative thing with this crowd. Come on. I want to introduce all of you to some people."

. . .

"AND YOU REMEMBER, KENDALL," Lacie said to Sophia more than forty minutes, several people, a Coke and a half, and a dozen hors d'oeuvres later.

Sophia smiled and gave the other woman a firm nod, her shyness long since dissipated. Lacie had affected the same hand at the small of the back touch she'd used in her condo though, something she was still hyperconscious of. She was sure Kendall picked up on it, too.

"Hi again," Kendall said. "Sophia, this is my wife, Chris." She nodded at the beautiful woman with a warm smile standing next to her.

"Nice to meet you." She offered her hand.

"Likewise," Chris said, as she took Sophia's hand. "Kendall mentioned you just the other day. I take it you haven't been with Tech Success long?"

"Oh, I don't work for Tech Success at all. I work with the Sun Valley Community Rec Center where Lacie is, er... "

"I'm sure Kendall has filled her in—" Lacie started to say.

"Where Lacie is doing a cute little project with a parade float," Heaven volunteered, as she glided over to their group in a sparkling silver jumpsuit only she or a drag queen could love.

Lacie dropped her hand from Sofia's back.

"Nice getup," Kendall offered. "Are you part of the entertainment later?"

Heaven's brows knitted. "Entertainment? There's a DJ... "

Chris rolled her eyes and mouthed the word 'dense' at Sofia.

"A few of the crew from Sun Valley are here, Heaven," Lacie said. "I've been introducing them around to all the people they'll be working with on projects going forward. Is there anyone you think we should talk to?"

Heaven preened at being asked for her input. Kendall shot Lacie an odd look that Sofia caught. The silver lamé clad woman missed it as she started reeling off names.

"Thanks," Lacie said to her. "You've mentioned a couple I hadn't thought of."

"Oh, my pleasure. I can certainly take Sophia here off your hands and introduce her around if you like." She gave Sophia a smile that didn't quite reach her eyes.

Lacie was quick to decline. "It's okay. We've already talked with a few of those folks."

"Yes. Thanks," Sophia managed.

Something caught Heaven's attention and she fluttered away, on to her next targets.

"What the hell was that all about?" Kendall asked, her question directed at Lacie. "Why is she being so fake nice?"

"Beats me."

Chris put in, "It seems to me like she's still got some designs on you, and she wants to put herself between you and Sophia here."

Sophia was taken aback by Chris's assumption. "Oh. No. We're not a couple." She waved a hand between herself and Lacie.

"Could have fooled us, sweetie," Kendall said.

I see where Lacie picked 'sweetie' up.

"You two are cute together and it's good to see her taking an interest in someone or something other than working for a change," Chris said.

"She, uh... she sort of had to," Sophia said.

Lacie nodded in agreement.

Kendall gave her appraisal, "At first, maybe. Not anymore."

Ted wandered up with Will's wife, Jeanette, following. "They're ready," he said to Lacie.

Sofia looked at Jeanette. "Where's Will?" When she got a coy half shrug in return, she turned to Lacie. "Who's ready? What's going on?"

A man she hadn't been introduced to picked up a micro-phone off the DJ stand and asked for everyone's attention.

"Hi, I'm Steve, for those of you who don't know me," he announced to the room.

Lacie bent to Sophia's ear and whispered, "Our CEO."

"We have clients all over Denver, across the state, across the country and even in some far-flung corners of the world. We appreciate them all. One of the ways we like to show our appre-ciation is by giving back when and where we can. This year brought us some significant challenges."

Heads nodded around the room.

"It really did, but we got through them together, came out stronger, and we're not wavering in our commitment to give back." He paused and took a sip from a water glass then picked up where he left off, "We have one more challenge; a new oppor-tunity to help a community organization this year. It came up very recently, only a couple of days ago, as a matter of fact. When you meet these folks, I know you'll want to get involved and help them like I do. Now, without further ado, I'd like to introduce you to William Ellison, the director of the Sun Valley Community Recreation Center and some of his young charges there."

Will stepped through a doorway located behind where Steve stood, joined him, and waved at the assembled crowd. Clevon, Whitney, DeMarco and Maya filed out too and lined up beside Will.

"We've been hiding these kids in the kitchen for about an hour," Steve said. "So, if all the cookies have been eaten up, you know why."

Clevon took a bow and the crowd laughed.

"How did the kids get here?" Sophia asked Lacie, who was on her left.

Jeanette answered from her right side, "They came with Will and I. Lacie set it all up."

Sophia's head shot back around to look at Lacie. "You did this?"

The other woman bowed at the waist, as Clevon had moments before.

"I don't know what to say... "

Lacie took her hand. "You don't have to say anything."

18

THANKSGIVING

Thanksgiving Day, Thursday, November 28th
Denver, Colorado

L acie woke up on Thanksgiving Day feeling more alone than she'd felt in all the years since she'd left Oklahoma. Since she was off, she'd spent most of the day Wednesday helping at the center with the kids who were all off school and primed for mischief. With the float done, it had been a task to keep them busy and focused and she'd returned home exhausted but happy. Now, she just felt empty.

She turned on the Macy's parade and watched the dancers performing in Herald Square while the parade made its way along the route. The music and spectacle lifted her mood a little until the camera panned the crowd and she saw all the children there with their families, watching. She felt a pang of longing in her chest she'd never felt before.

She turned the television off and lolled her head back on the sofa, thinking. *I've got to get out of here. Do something.* Her thoughts turned to Sofia. *What's she doing today?*

She hadn't mentioned any Thanksgiving plans and Lacie didn't pry, figuring it would be all about family for the Vaca's.

An hour later, showered and dressed, she headed into the city. She drove past the rec center and a couple of more blocks to the church they'd arranged to borrow tables and chairs from for the center Christmas Eve celebration.

A line was forming just off the parking lot at a side door that wasn't open. The people stood waiting, laughing, and talking, seemingly impervious to the cold. Some were neatly dressed. Some were disheveled. She willed herself to make no assumptions about any of them.

She went around to the back side of the building where she found a door propped open, the smell of roasting turkey wafting out. *It's been a long time since I've smelled that.*

Stepping into the massive church kitchen that was a hive of activity brought back memories of working in the dining hall in college on a work/study program that was part of her scholarship agreement.

"We won't be serving for about 90 minutes yet," a man in a priest's collar who was carrying a massive bowl of cranberry sauce told her as he squeezed by between her and the workers at the worktable in front of her, with their backs to her.

The two women turned, both smiling. One said, "There's probably already a line forming outside dear. If you give me a moment, I can show you where."

"There is," Lacie said, "but I'm not here to eat. I'm here to help. To volunteer."

"Oh. I'm so sorry," the other woman began. She wiped her hands on a towel looped through the belt of her apron. "I don't recall seeing you before. Are you on the sign-up roster?" She waved a hand. "Not that it really matters. We always seem to have lots of extra volunteers."

"That's good, right? I mean, I guess it's good."

"It is, dear. It is. Let's just get you settled." She motioned for Lacie to follow her and led her into a cloakroom. "This is makeshift for the volunteers today, so you don't have to worry about your things. Most of these folks just want a decent meal and no trouble, you understand, but—" She shook her head. "There's always the potential for a bad apple."

Lacie took her coat off and hung it up.

The woman handed her a clipboard. "I'm Marie. I'm in charge of keeping track of everyone. I just need you to print your name and then sign right here." She pointed at an empty line.

"Lacie. Nice to meet you, Marie."

When she finished filling in her line, Marie cut to the chase. "What are you good at, Lacie? Do you cook?"

"Some, but I can certainly cut, chop, peel, slice and dice."

"Well then, there's a whole lot of that going on! Follow me."

She led Lacie back into the kitchen, taking her toward the front and the serving line area. She bypassed all of that, saying, "All the food will be up here starting in about an hour. Most of us will rotate up to help serve."

She took a right at the end of the line and walked down the row between the massive industrial stoves on the left and prep tables on the right. "Every oven has a turkey in it, all in various stages. We'll server for about four hours. A few will come out soon, other, smaller ones that don't take as much time will go in."

About halfway down the line, she put her hand on the shoulder of a woman wearing a chef's hat but otherwise dressed for the high heat of a kitchen working at full capacity. "This is the big boss, Eva Vaca. What she says is gospel around here."

Eva's knife stopped and she half turned toward Marie. She did a double take when she saw Lacie. The first words out of her mouth were, "Did Sofia ask you to come?"

"Is she here? I mean, I came on my own. I had no idea you, or she would be here today."

"Yes, she's here and Hector is, too. We do this every year."

I'm not at all surprised.

"They're out setting the tables. You might want to help them."

She resisted the urge to swallow. "I can help anywhere you need me. Here in the kitchen is fine."

Marie nudged her elbow and whispered, "Gospel."

"Or I can help with the tables... "

Eva cracked a smile. It wasn't big, but it put Lacie more at ease. She waved a hand down the row of tables. "If you can stand the heat, Charlene could use some help down there with the starches."

Heat. "Starches. Got it."

She spent the next forty minutes dicing previously peeled potatoes to go into the massive boiling pots for real mashed potatoes. *No instant stuff here!*

LACIE TOOK up a position in front of the stuffing right next to Sofia who was ladling gravy.

Sofia glanced her way. "I can't believe you're here. Is this part of your... you know?"

"No."

"Then why are you here?"

"You mentioned it before, and I remembered. I just wanted to come, to help. No ulterior motives."

"Not even brownie points?" she asked through her smile for the man standing in front of her holding his plate out.

"With you? No. I honestly didn't know you were going to be here. You only told me why the center would be closed today."

"This is our church. We've been doing this on Thanksgiving for as long as I can remember."

"Ah." *That tells me a lot.* "It's a nice tradition."

AN HOUR LATER, Lacie's feet were killing her, but there was no way she was going to give up on the job. Standing next to Sofia, chatting and joking with her and all the people coming through felt uplifting. She knew the situation was dire for some of the people, but she also knew some were there more for fellowship than need. And several of the kids from the center had come through.

Clevon escorted his grandmother Elizabeth through the line, helping her to carry her plate and fetching things she couldn't carry or forgot. She saw a new side of the teenager, a sight she wouldn't trade for anything.

DeMarco and his mom showed up, too. When she saw Lacie, she tried to reach over the line to hug her, thanking her over and over for her help and a job with full benefits, even for a part-timer.

Her right side felt electric. She could feel the love, the care, and the strength emanating from the younger woman next to her. *She's always been amazing to me, but wow.*

A shiver ran up her spine when Sofia bumped her. Her loins tingled. She stopped mid scoop and excused herself to turn away for a second to gather her bearings. *Get it together, Lacie. This is a church. A Catholic church, at that.*

"Sorry," Sofia said. Her eyes gleamed.

"No, you're not," Lacie responded. The younger woman just smiled, but she remained a bit closer than she had been.

Sweat ran down Lacie's back, but it wasn't from the heat of the ovens.

THEY SAT in the small break area set aside for the staff. When the only other volunteer in there eating picked up his empty plate and left, Sofia said to Lacie, "Did I tell you my mom had a plate waiting for me in the oven when I got home the night my car got broken into?"

"The night we ate at Torchy's?"

Sofia nodded.

"You didn't eat again, did you?"

"No, I didn't. I told her you took me out."

"Oh."

"She didn't ask any questions."

"Hmm."

"She didn't get mad either."

"Did you expect her to?"

"Sort of."

"She didn't say anything?"

"Well, yeah. She asked me what I wanted for my lunch the next day while she transferred the food she'd kept warm for me from a plate to containers."

I don't even know where to go with that.

Sofia leaned closer. "Lacie, I'm twenty-two... an adult. It's time I started to act like one."

Lacie drew in a deep breath. *Where are we going with this?*

"It's time I stopped being afraid of what she thinks. What I mean is, I wanted to tell you, I'm starting to—"

Hector walked into the room saying, "I finally got a break, too. Your mother, she's a tough taskmaster!"

· · ·

LACIE STOOD with Hector and Sofia in the parking lot while they waited for Eva to finish her last round of kitchen checks.

"I'm tired," Hector said, "but it's a good kind of tired."

Sofia was bouncing on the balls of her feet. "I'm not. I actually feel a little keyed up."

"I wish I was that young, with that much energy," Lacie said. "I'm not totally exhausted, but I'm not raring to go either."

Hector flipped a hand at her. "You're too young to be acting like an old one like me."

Lacie coughed as Sofia said, "Dad, you're only forty-five."

"It's a lot different from thirty, though," he said as he tipped his head at Lacie.

"I'm forty, Hector."

He looked her up and down. "Nah, I don't buy it."

"I'm flattered, but it's true."

He winked at her. "Whatever you say. Why don't we just keep that between us?"

"Um... okay? Can I ask why?"

Instead of answering, he asked, "How's that parade float coming?"

Sofia answered, "It's pretty much done except for the last-minute stuff we can't do until we get it over to the parade route."

Eva came out the back door just then.

"All set, my love, my queen?" Hector asked her.

Lacie and Sofia both laughed at the unexpected endearments, but Eva beamed. "Te amo, mi rey."

"A good day," she said as she turned toward her daughter and Lacie. "We served 427 people, not counting volunteers."

"That's amazing, mama," Sofia said.

Hector put an arm around his wife. "I'm taking you home where you can soak your feet and relax with a nice cup of coffee."

"That sounds nice, but I'm making the coffee first." She

looked again at Sofia and Lacie. "He couldn't make a decent cup of coffee if his life depended on it." She gave him a little poke in the stomach.

"Hey! I resemble that remark."

Sofia and Lacie laughed again at their banter.

Hector had another trick up his sleeve. "The girls here were just telling me about the parade float. They've got all kinds of energy left and they were thinking of heading over to the center while it's quiet to do some finishing up."

Lacie's eyes widened involuntarily in surprise at his fib, but she did her best to recover as he asked her, "You'll run Sofia home later, won't you?"

"Um, yes. Of course."

"WHAT WAS THAT ALL ABOUT?" Lacie asked Sofia, as she reversed out of the parking spot.

"I have no idea. I've never known my father to lie like that."

Lacie turned out onto the street. "He might have wanted some time alone with your mom."

"Or, maybe he thinks that's what we want." Sofia said softly.

Lacie glanced over at her, but she had to turn her focus back to the road. "Is that what you want?" She mentally crossed her fingers as she waited for the answer.

Sofia half turned to face her and said, her voice firm, "Yes."

Sofia

THE BED WAS as soft and as comfortable as Sofia imagined it would be. She laid back and watched through hooded eyes as Lacie started the fireplace going, dimmed the lights, and moved back to the bedside. She sat at Sophia's waist and leaned over, bringing their faces close. "You're sure?"

She gave her a slight nod, as she answered her like she had in the car, "Yes."

Lacie bent low and claimed her lips in a soft kiss.

Sofia writhed beneath her as the other woman took her time, only beginning to lick and nip at her lower lip after several long seconds. She couldn't help the low moan she let out when she let the tip of Lacie's tongue gain the entrance it sought.

Lacie reached around her back and pulled her up into a sitting position, pulling their upper bodies together.

"It's been so long," Sofia whispered. She dropped backwards again and tried to tug Lacie along with her, but Lacie tensed a little and held her position.

"I don't want to hurt you. You're so... tiny," Lacie whispered.

The mood temporarily broken; Sofia chuckled. "Short, yes. Tiny, no. I've been called stocky, husky, and sturdy, but never tiny."

Lacie ran a hand down her arm, moved in toward her hip and down her leg. She shivered at the touch.

"I love every curvy inch of you," Lacie said.

Sophia picked up on her use of the "L" word and smiled. She tugged at the older, taller woman again. "Come down here. I need to feel you against me." She claimed her soon to be lover's lips again in another kiss as Lacie shifted position, moving over her and then beside her.

Before she could complain, Lacie rolled her toward herself and molded their entire bodies together, then took her lips in another searing kiss.

As Lacie trailed kisses down her neck, Sophia could feel the heat rising from her core. The fire, their clothing, their closeness, it was all too much to bear. She pulled back a little and began undoing the buttons of her blouse.

Lacie stilled her hands, then took over the task herself. She made short work of Sophia's bra too, then sat up and quickly removed her own garments.

Sophia bucked when Lacie positioned herself over her, allowing their breasts to barely touch before she returned to kissing the curve of her neck. *No better. Still too hot to handle.* She groaned as the other woman rose up off her, but the kissing and licking moved lower. *No. It was better. I need to feel her.*

She reached her arms around Lacie's neck and ran her hands to the middle of her back, tugging her down. "I need to feel you. All of you."

Lacie sank down, giving in. She reclaimed Sophia's lips.

Sophia moaned at the feel of full contact. Her nipples strained against the breasts of the other woman. Her clit throbbed. She wrapped her hands around Lacie's backside and pulled her in tight as she raised her own hips off the bed, looking for some friction to relieve her tortured core.

Lacie kept up her assault on Sophia's mouth, but she shifted her hips to get a knee between Sophia's legs.

Sophia tossed her head, breaking their kiss. As Lacie moved her knee about, it was all she could do to pant for air. The sensation was incredible. When the older woman replaced her knee with a hand and began stroking her folds and her clit, she lost the ability to think.

19

THE MORNING AFTER

*T*his *isn't going to be easy*, Lacie thought, as they both dressed. *She's so young, and I know she's going to have doubts.* She pushed her own thoughts aside about how any such relationship between them was going to work. *One day at a time. You've been primarily single for a long time.*

The fireplace was still on. In the flickering light, she caught a glimpse of Sofia's face. Her tan colored skin over her cheekbones was flushed with a hint of red after their lovemaking.

Lovemaking. There's a word. It was sex with Heaven. It was so much more with Sophia. She swallowed back a sigh. *I hope I'm doing the right thing. I don't know how to be someone's girlfriend anymore.*

Sophia finished dressing and walked over to her. She surprised her when she pulled her into a quick, chaste hug. "Thank you, for being so gentle and... just thank you." the curvy, raven-haired beauty said.

Gentle? I did try to hold back. A little. For a minute. Lacie looped her arms around Sophia's waist, dipped her head, and kissed the tip of the shorter woman's nose. "You haven't done this much, have you?" She asked her question softly, not meaning to offend, but she felt Sophia stiffen.

"Was it bad?" she asked as she tried to pull away.

Lacie reeled her back in and kissed her. A few long seconds later, she drug her lips away and said, "It was amazing."

Sophia gave her a half smile then put her hands on Lacie's chest and pushed off. "I hate to do this, but I should be getting home."

"It's okay. Just let me find my boots and we can go." *Baby steps. She might be willing to push back a little against Eva, but she's not ready to have a sleepover.*

As she wandered toward the front door where she was pretty sure she'd divested herself of her boots when they'd come in wrapped in each other, she thought of Eva along with Sophia. *Not sure where I want this to go, but it'll go nowhere fast if I can't win Eva over. She might have thawed toward me a little personally today, but that's before she could be sure I'd corrupted her little girl.* She shook herself, warding off the thought of Sofia as a girl. *She's young, but she's a woman, Lacie. A wonderful woman and one worth fighting for.*

"You okay?" Sofia asked.

She pulled the other woman's coat off the rack on the back of the door and held it open for her to step into. "Lovely. I'm just wonderful." She pulled the door open and swung her arm out with a flourish. "Milady, your carriage awaits."

SHE HELD Sofia's hand as she drove and stole an occasional glance her way. When Sofia caught her looking, she gave her a smile and a quick squeeze of the hand.

Look at me. In a couple of weeks I've gone from not wanting a relationship with anyone to wondering what this beautiful young woman sees in me; why she wants to be with me. I've gone from thinking about a future full of work, to a future that I hope includes her. She plead with the universe. *Please, let it include her. What if she finds her wings and flies?* She let out a small sigh.

"Hmm?" Sofia asked.

"Sorry. Just realizing how tired I am."

"Now I'm the sorry one. We shouldn't have... I shouldn't have pushed you to—"

Bad choice of words, moron. She interrupted, saying, "Sofia, no. It's been a long day, yes, but you didn't push me into anything I didn't want." She was on a straight stretch of road. She held the wheel steady with her left hand and turned her head to face the other woman. As she gave Sophia her most fiery look, she raised their clasped hands to her lips and kissed the one she held.

SOFIA SPOKE as Lacie stopped in the driveway at the ranch. "Thanks for bringing me home."

She shut off the engine. "My pleasure."

Sofia looked at the keys now dangling from Lacie's hand. "I know you're tired. You don't have to hang around if you don't want to."

Lacie couldn't read her eyes. *I can't tell if she's being supportive or if she's afraid I might come in.* "We could compromise, and I could walk you to the door. No public displays of affection, I promise." She drew a finger in an 'X' across her heart.

Sofia gave her a small smile. "Then you better kiss me now."

"As you wish, Milady." She bent toward the now chuckling beauty and claimed her lips in a quick peck.

"I think you can do better than that," she was informed.

"And if your mother is watching from the window?"

"She can't see at this angle."

"I see. Tested that, have you?"

"Me? No. That would have been Carlotta, my sister. I just took good mental notes."

"Ah. Where does she live? I was surprised not to meet her today."

"Her husband is in the military. They're in Japan - Okinawa - right now. They probably won't be home for Christmas this year either."

"Oh, that's got to be hard on your parents, not seeing them and the grandkids... they have kids, right?"

Sophia nodded. "Two. And yes, it is hard on them, mom especially... " She shrugged. Let's not talk about them right now. She snaked a hand back around Lacie's neck. "About that kiss..."

Lacie let the Sofia pull her closer and gave her what she was asking for, only dragging her lips away when things threatened to get heated again. "Let's get out and chill for a minute," she said. "I think we both need to cool off, you especially if your mother is waiting up for you."

"I'm going to have to face her sometime."

"I've recently learned, from an unbelievably amazing woman, truth settles better in the light of day."

"Is that so?"

"It is."

As she drove away a few minutes later, Lacie made some silent resolutions. *I won't let her go it alone ever again. Not if I can help it. She may not need my help, but I need to make sure I'm there for her when she does.*

20

PARADE

Friday Night, December 6th
Parade of Lights
Denver, Colorado

S ofia rushed about with the staple gun, tacking up strings of small Christmas lights, being careful not to staple through the wires, as Will, Ted and Clevon set up the panels of the float. What they'd constructed fit inside the center's multi-purpose room when it was fully assembled, but all put together it was too high to fit out the double doors which opened into the back alley. They'd purposely assembled their creation it in parts.

Lacie followed her around the trailer, holding the box of extra staples, the wood glue, and a small claw hammer in case she needed anything. "This is really going to be something."

Will shot her a look. "Who sounds excited like one of the kids now?"

"She's never seen the parade, Will." Sofia said, reminding him of Lacie's admission.

Ted stopped working and stared. "Seriously?"

Lacie shrugged. "I'm not originally from around here. It never crossed my radar before."

Sophia spoke over her shoulder as she positioned the staple gun, "I've got to wonder what other things you don't know about this area."

"Probably a lot. But I can learn. I've certainly learned quite a bit in the past month."

"This is true," Will said.

Sofia put a couple more staples in and called out, "Done! Light it up!"

Clevon jumped in to do the job he'd been assigned on the route, but Will put out a hand to hold him off. "Not yet, bud. Let's wait until we get the thumbs up from Ted and do it all at once, lights, music, everything."

The teenager backed off, saying, "We still have too much daylight, anyway. It'll be better in the dark."

"We've got to get it to the parade route lineup before dark," Lacie reminded them. "We're going to have to step it up."

Sofia gave her girlfriend a poke when she thought no one else was looking before walking away and tossing over her shoulder, "You do sound as excited as one of the kids."

Ted kneeled down and made one more wiring connection to the power source he'd rigged up, then stood. "Okay," he said as he worked his way through the structure and off the back of the trailer, "Clevon, go ahead and do your thing. I'd rather fix any problems now rather than when it's dark." He, Will, and Sophia stood to one side near the front end of the trailer on the driver's side.

Lacie rushed over to the group as Clevon threw a single switch for the lights that would stay on, and then the two switches he had to throw together to sync all the different pieces of the rope lights with the music.

Sofia crossed her fingers and held her breath. *Please work. Please work!*

All the lights that were supposed to come on with the first switch appeared to. Ted stepped away from the group and made it to the end of the trailer, checking things out before the music rose and the other lights started to come on and go off with the beat of the music.

Smiles spread across their faces as they listened to the first strains of a stanza of 'I'll be Home for Christmas' and watched the slow scroll of the lights. When the beat picked up with 'Wonderful Christmas Time,' the lights danced a bit faster. By 'Jingle Bell Rock,' they were flashing fast, and the rec center crew was cheering.

Will joined Ted on his walk around, a hand on his shoulder, heaping praise on him. "You did it. You pulled it off! This is so amazing! I don't know how to thank you."

Still shy, even though he'd been around regularly at the center, Ted blushed.

Lacie rushed the two men and raised a hand toward her co-worker. "High-five! You rocked it. Great job, Ted."

Will dropped his hand off Ted's shoulder and advanced toward Lacie. "Just warning you, I'm about to hug you. You were a big part of making this happen." He pulled her into a bear hug as he went on, "It never would have been like this without you. Thank you. From the bottom of my heart, thank you. And, if they don't say it, know that the kids thank you too."

OVER AT THE parade staging area, as day turned into night and the kids started to arrive, the excitement built. They all wanted to see their creation fully lit, but Sophia, Will, and Lacie held them in check. They'd light it and let them walk around and see it all before they had to be in their places and roll out on their cue to join the parade.

It's going to be a good night, Sophia thought.

Will tapped Sophia's shoulder and pointed up the line at the floats ahead of them. "Judges."

"What?"

"The judges. They're working their way down the line. We should probably get ready to light up so we can hit it when they get here."

"Wow," Sophia said. "I hadn't even thought about judging. We've never had a 'real' float before." She made air quotes.

Lacie grinned. "Now you do."

Will clapped his hands together and called out to the children, "Find your places everyone."

Maya tugged Lacie's hand. "Is it time to start?"

"Almost," Lacie said, as she bent and picked the little girl up. She carried her over to her seat on the float where she explained to her and all the kids in earshot, "Let's see those pretty smiles everyone. Some people are going to come around and check out your float in a minute. Maybe you'll win a trophy later on, if they really like it."

"What's a trophy?" Maya asked.

Sophia, who had followed behind, laughed, but the laughter died on her tongue when she caught a whiff of a familiar perfume. She turned to her right in time to see Heaven sidle up on the other side of Lacie, lean in and whisper something to her.

Sophia bristled, but Lacie seemed to take the semi-private overture in stride. She turned slightly toward the other woman, shook her hand, and said, "Glad you could make it."

She invited her?

Heaven looked around Lacie to Sophia. "Hi there. I hope you

don't mind if I tag along today. After seeing you all at the party the other night, I really want to help."

Tag along and do what? The work is done.

"I'll do whatever you need."

Will said as he passed by, "We could really use someone to walk along opposite Sophia and pass out a few fliers as we go down the parade route.

"Sure," Heaven said. "I don't mind the walk." She glanced down at her footwear, another pair of over-the-knee boots with three-inch heels. "Oh, but... " She waved a hand at them.

"I'll do that, Will," Lacie said. "She can ride in the truck with you and throw candy... er, if that's okay?"

"Oh, now that sounds like fun! And, it sounds a lot warmer." With that, she turned on a heel, moved to the cab of the pickup, and climbed in.

"I hate to do that to you, Will," Lacie said by way of apology, "but Sophia, Ted, and I can handle the float and the kids. She'd just be in the way and trying to take credit where none is due."

Sophia let out the breath she didn't realize she'd been holding. *My feelings exactly.*

AS THEY APPROACHED the review stand, the music cycled back to, 'I'll be Home for Christmas.' The rope lights strobed along in time, the thoughts of the children about what home meant to them, lighting in patterns.

"Entry number 47," the parade announcer called out, "The Sun Valley Community Recreation Center is the winner of the best civic or government entry award for their float, 'What Home Means to Me.' Isn't it amazing, folks?" He swung an arm out at their twinkling mobile house as the crowd applauded. A volunteer reached down and handed a trophy to Sophi as she walked past.

Sophia held the trophy out to the kids nearest to her. "This is a trophy, Maya." She let the little girl and a couple of others close to her touch it, then nodded at Clevon to take it.

"Hold it up!" Lacie called to him from the other side of the float. "Let everyone see it."

The teenager hoisted their prize in the air, a grin spreading across his face.

CLEVON WAS STILL GRINNING and still holding the trophy when they stopped and dismounted several minutes later.

Heaven put a hand on the boy's arm. "Aren't you just the cutest thing? And, you look so good holding that."

Sophia didn't think it was possible, but the teen's smile broadened even more as he preened at her praise.

He held the trophy out. "This is for all the little people."

"Clevon!" Will called out as Heaven laughed.

"What? They are little." He pointed at the younger kids, but then flashed his smile at Heaven. "Except you. Right here, I mean."

"And funny too," Heaven cooed at him, oblivious to the looks Whitney, standing a few feet away, was giving the two of them.

"Awe, thanks."

"And polite."

Whitney advanced on the pair and waved a hand around. "Are we done with all this here, because we really should take some pictures, don't ya think?"

Sophia leaned into Lacie and whispered. "I think our boy has found his power."

"Heaven help us," Lacie said, then thought about it. "Sorry. Bad choice of words."

21

HORSE SENSE

Saturday Morning, December 7th

L acie stretched out in her bed. She turned her head slightly and peered at the narrow opening in the curtains over the doors out to the balcony. *Still dark.*

She stretched again and stood up. *We were later than expected getting everything back to the center and all locked up, but I promised. And, I really am looking forward to it. Part of it, anyway.*

SOFIA WAS WAITING on the front porch when she pulled in. She took a steadying breath as she stepped out of the car, a jangle of nerves welling up at the thought of having to face Eva Vaca. *Does she know?* She didn't dare ask Sophia. *I'm not sure if I'm better off knowing or not knowing.*

Sofia sketched a wave with a gloved hand and left the porch. "Hi 'ya. Unless you're wanting coffee, I thought we'd just go on over to the barn and get started.

Lacie stifled her sigh of relief. "Sounds good."

"Shouldn't take too long. I appreciate you agreeing to help. Britt usually works on Saturday, even when I'm at the center."

"I might be a little rusty," Lacie admitted. "It's been a while." *Years. Years and Years.*

"We're mainly feeding and mucking. The horses don't much care, as long as they get their feed and clean bedding."

"I think I can handle that." She followed Sophia to the main horse barn.

Lacie was surprised at the size of the barn and the number of stalls. "How many horses?"

"There are thirty-two or more in here at any given time. Sick ones, pregnant ones... other issues, there's a different barn."

"Wow. That's a lot."

"It's a big ranch. A lot of hands in the high season to manage a lot of heads of cattle."

"I didn't know it was so big."

Sofia laughed. "You know, for someone that's lived here as long as you have, you don't know a lot. This ranch is responsible for a good portion of the beef supply in Colorado."

"So, where are all these hands, then? Why are you and Britt usually left to do this all alone?"

Sofia pointed at baled hay stacked in an end stall. "We'll grab a few of those and give them each a flake in their door trough to get started on while I mix their feed." She shrugged. "And, as for your question, it all comes back to my dad. This is his domain. He's particular about who does what and how it gets done."

"And you want *me* to help?"

Sofia chuckled and bumped elbows with Lacie. "You'll be fine."

· · ·

THE SUN WAS up over the horizon outside the breakfast nook window when Eva laid a plate with a fried egg, a fried plantain, and a thick slice of tomato on the scrubbed wood kitchen table in front of each of them. "I can make more eggs and plantains," Eva said to Sophia, "but your father was over excited at fresh garden tomato this morning."

Lacie shot Sophia a questioning look.

"There's a greenhouse on the property," she explained. "Mom tends to it." To her mother she said, "This is fine, Mom. Thank you."

"Yes, thank you. This looks really great, Mrs. Vaca."

Sophia shook her head. "You can call her Eva."

No, I don't think I can. Eva Vaca gave a quick nod of her head but turned away from the table without saying if she was acknowledging their thanks or if it was okay for Lacie to call her Eva. Lacie thought, I'm not taking any chances there.

She asked Sophia, "So what's the rest of a Saturday workday like around here?"

"For me, there's not much now until this afternoon. Dad has to make a run to the feed mill. Some of the ranch hands will help him unload what he brings back. I'll need to be on hand then to inventory it and make sure it gets put away right, but that doesn't take very long." She was quiet for a minute as she took a bite of her plantain. "Can you hang around for a while longer, though? After breakfast, I mean?"

Lacie pointed at her coffee mug. "Is there more of that?"

"Yes. There's always plenty of coffee, even in the summer. I swear it's what Dad has instead of blood in his veins."

"Then, yes. I can. What do you need me to do?"

"I thought we could talk about the party plans. Get some of the specifics down."

Eva showed up at the edge of the four-person table with the carafe from the coffeemaker in hand. She topped off Lacie's cup while Sophia broached the party subject again for her mother's benefit. "Are you able to help with the decorations and serving at the party this year, Mama?"

"Of course."

"Did you want to help with some of the planning?"

Eva waved a hand dismissively. "I'll leave that to you all. But, shouldn't you be doing that with Will?"

The elder Vaca woman's tone told Lacie Eva didn't approve of them cutting the center director out of their planning session. "She's right. We should wait. We want Britt to be involved too."

Sophia's face fell.

Lacie couldn't stand to see her disappointed. "Although, there are a couple of things we could talk about right now that don't directly involve them and the party."

Sophia sat back, more at ease. Eva stood with the coffee carafe poised over her daughter's cup, listening too.

"Will told me the check from Tech success came through. We'll have to start planning the shopping, too, but remember when I was asking some of the kids what they would like for Christmas that doesn't cost much?" She only paused for a beat. "Most of them wanted things that were experiences that didn't require more than a little of someone's time."

"Right," Sophia said. "I heard Clevon say he wants to go fishing."

Lacie bobbed her head. "Yes, and I talked to Will about it. He's all for the idea of someone taking him, but he doesn't fish himself. Neither do I." She looked away from Sophia, to Eva. "Does Hector fish?"

Eva started pouring coffee, slowly. "He does from time to time. Summer is hard. That's high season around here. He does like to ice fish this time of year, but no one really likes to go with him to do that. Too cold."

"That's perfect, though!" Lacie said. "He could fish one on

one with Clevon. That's what the boy really needs. Some man-to-man time. Do you think he'd do it?"

Eva stopped pouring and set the pot down carefully. "You'd have to ask him, but I imagine. He loves doing things for that center and for those kids."

"I'll do that."

Sofia held up a hand. "Why don't you let me handle that?"

"Well…" Lacie said.

Sofia's eyes narrowed and she cocked her head to give Lacie her best 'what did you do now' look. "What?"

"It's not bad," Lacie said, as she waggled a hand toward her girlfriend. "There's another child I'd like to ask him about. It's Maya. She really wants to ride a horse. This is a ranch… with horses. Do you think—"

"It's a working ranch," Eva said firmly.

"Yes, true Mom," Sophia put in, "but they've given trail rides here before."

Eva's response was no nonsense. "To cattle customers, Sofia. The buyers, as your father calls them. Not to children."

"It wouldn't even have to be a trail ride," Lacie said. "Let her spend a few minutes helping you feed them like we did this morning. Possibly help her mount one and trot it around in the corral. She's only six. It wouldn't take much to make her happy."

Sofia eyed Lacie. "Let me talk to my dad, see what he says. Hopefully we'll be able to work something out, if not here, then with one of the therapy ranches."

"Won't they charge?" Lacie asked.

"They might, but maybe not. Let's wait and see what Dad says first."

. . .

LACIE WASHED HER HANDS, then ran one of the wet ones through her hair to give it a little spike before drying both on a hand towel. *The hat did me no favors out there.*

She opened the door of the tiny powder room and stepped out into the hallway, away from the sound of the still running commode. She could hear Sophia and her mother talking in the kitchen.

She opened her mouth to speak as she began to move back in their direction, but she stopped short and stood still to listen in when she heard Eva say, "And just what are your feelings for Lacie?"

It was silent for several long seconds before Sophia responded, "She's just a friend, Mom. Nothing more, nothing less. She's here today and she'll be gone tomorrow."

Lacie didn't wait to hear more. She rushed through the hallway and ducked her head into the kitchen. She held up her cell phone. "Sorry. Gotta run. Kendall has some sort of emergency. Really sorry." She didn't bother to wait for a response, instead turning on her heel and heading down the hallway the other way to the front door.

She was in her Subaru and pulling away by the time Sophia reached the front porch. The younger woman waved an arm her way, trying to get her attention. Lacie saw the gesture, but she ignored it.

Sophia

EVA JOINED her daughter on the porch. "That didn't go well, did it?"

"Pardon?"

"She obviously heard us talking."

Sophia's look was stricken. *Oh my. What have I done?*

Eva took her daughter's hand and tugged her toward the door. "It's time for us to have a chat, clear the air, but not out here. This cold air might be good for the soul, but not the lungs."

FROM HER PLACE at one end of the sofa, Eva began, "Why don't you tell me what's really going on here?"

From the other end of the couch, Sofia deflected the question. "I'm not sure what you mean." *I know exactly what you mean, but I also know you don't really want to hear it.*

"With Lacie."

Sophia sighed.

"You lied to me a few minutes ago. You never lie to me, not to my face."

"I've never lied to you at all, Mom." She met her mother's eyes and saw something in them she'd never seen. "At least, not... Not until a few minutes ago," she admitted.

"Omission is lying too."

"Pardon?"

"I know you're... Well, let's just say that I know you prefer women, Sofia. I knew about your freshman college roommate."

Sofia swallowed hard. "I... I don't know what to say." She cast about, unable to meet her mother's eyes. "How... how did you know?"

"A mother knows. I could see the way you looked at her; the way she looked at you. You look at Lacie the same way; maybe even more intense."

Sofia was silent.

"And, she looks at you the same way, you look at her."

I want to believe that, but I can't. "No, Mom."

Eva Vaca shook her head. "She does, and I know you see that. If you don't see it, you're lying to yourself."

She didn't realize she'd been holding her breath. She let the air out and sucked in another gulp as multiple responses played out in her mind. She decided it was time for the truth. All of it. "I was in a relationship with my roommate, back then. It's true."

"And you broke it off because of me." Eva's tone was matter of fact.

The younger woman nodded. "I knew you would never accept it."

"You never even talked to me. You used to talk to me about everything. Mid-way through your freshman year, you just stopped."

"I know." She was contrite. "I didn't think you really noticed. Not that. You were always so... busy."

"Sofia, I notice everything."

Boy, do I know it now.

"I certainly noticed that, and I realized fairly quickly why."

"You never said anything."

"It wasn't my place to."

"Does Dad know... did he know about that?"

"We never talked about it. He knows about Lacie, though. Your father has recently started lying to me too."

"No, Mom. He..." *She's right. He did lie to cover for me.*

"You don't need to defend him. I know why he did it."

"I'm so sorry."

Eva raised a hand, stopping her from saying more. "So, back to my original question. Just what are your feelings for Lacie?"

Sophia whispered, "I think I'm in love with her. No. That's not the truth either." She sat up straight. "I'm in love with her."

Eva dipped her head in acknowledgement of her daughter's words, but she didn't respond.

Sofia went on. "I didn't think she–or any woman–would ever meet with your approval. That's why I lied."

"She's a lot older than you. Old enough to be me–your mother, I mean–almost. That does concern me, but it's plain to me how you feel about each other. If it was one sided, that would be different. If you were chasing after her—"

"That's just it. That's what concerns me. We're so... different. We don't look at anything the same way. She's got years of experience over me, but I don't always agree with her critical eye. And, there's..." she trailed off.

Eva waited her out while she gathered her thoughts.

"Can I ask you a question?"

Eva nodded.

"Do you ever feel like you're subservient to dad?"

The elder Vaca woman sat back hard into the corner of the sofa. "Do you really think that?"

Her mother's incredulous tone made Sofia wish she could take the question back. " didn't mean to upset you... again. I just... I see how you are with him. The things you do for him. I can't be that sort of person and sometimes I feel like, because I'm so much younger than Lacie—"

"I do things for him because I want to do them, Sofia. We both work very hard. We *all* work hard here. My job is to make sure my family is cared for so my family members can do their jobs. I love what I do."

That's sort of what Dad said. Sofia gave her mother a smile.

"Does Lacie make you feel like you must serve her?"

Sofia shook her head. "No."

"That's something to think about then, isn't it?" She didn't wait for a response, saying instead, "Your father will be off to the feed mill soon. If you want to make things right with Lacie, I suggest you reach out to her or go to her, but don't forget you need to be back here. There's work to be done and you agreed to do it."

"Yes, Ma'am."

LACIE DIDN'T ANSWER her phone. Torn, Sofia looked at her watch. She had about an hour and a half once her dad pulled out.

She pulled on a coat, went out and walked halfway to the barn until she could see where the truck and trailer were usually parked. The big Ford diesel was sitting there idling. *He'll be leaving any minute.*

She raced back to the driveway, jumped in her car, and willed it to start quickly. She gave it only a minute to warm up before she pulled out and headed to Lacie's condo. *I hope she went home. Please!*

22

COMING TO HER SENSES

Lacie

S he's too young. You knew that! Lacie pounded the steering wheel. *She's not ready for this. She's not ready to actually come out into the open. She's afraid of her mother and she's not going to get over that anytime soon. She may never get over that.*

Lacie pulled into her driveway and stopped, not bothering to hit the opener for the garage. She got out and marched to her front door without a thought, but then fumbled for the appropriate key since she rarely used the door from the outside.

Her cell phone buzzed again in her hand.

SOPHIA: We need to talk.

I DON'T KNOW what to say to you. It buzzed again. This time, it wasn't Sophia.

. . .

KENDALL: "WHERE ARE YOU?"

SHE PUSHED her front door open and stepped inside, where she removed a glove so she could respond.

LACIE: Just got home. What's up?
    Kendall: Home? Out all night, were you?
    Lacie: No.

WHY WOULD SHE THINK THAT? Lacie looked at her watch. *Ah. Just after 9:00 AM.*

LACIE: I was out at the Vaca Ranch helping out.
    Kendall: Getting cozy with the parents, are you?
    Lacie: Ha. No, not hardly.
    Kendall: Trouble in paradise?

LACIE DIDN'T KNOW what to say to that, either. She laid the phone down on an end table near the front door and shucked off her boots. She inspected the carpet on the way back to put them by the door, hoping she hadn't tracked in anything from the barns in her fumbling around to get into the condo.

The phone buzzed again. *I don't know how to answer that, Kendall.* She picked it up.

. . .

KENDALL: Want to come over for brunch in a bit? Talk about it?

Lacie: No, sorry. I already ate and I'm whipped. I think I'm going to head back to bed for a few.

Kendall: Suit yourself. If you wake up in a couple of hours hungry, come on over.

SHE HUNG up her coat and inspected her clothes. Her shirt and jeans were clean. Satisfied, she headed to the stairs. About three stairs up, there was a knock at the door.

Who could that be? Deep down, she knew.

She was right. Sophia stood outside on the tiny stoop. She swung the door wide and stood aside. "It's still pretty cold. You better come in."

"Thank you," Sofia said softly. She took a deep breath. "I won't take up a lot of your time. I just came to say I'm sorry...to try and clear the air."

Lacie closed the door but didn't offer to take Sophia's coat. Instead, she walked over to her sofa and sat down. "You don't have anything to be sorry for."

Sofia moved toward her. "I do. I know you heard what I said to my mother."

Lacie tried to stifle a reaction as she watched the younger woman.

Sofia swayed nervously from foot to foot. "I... I lied to her, Lacie. I told her I didn't have feelings for you, and I know you heard that, and that's why you left."

"So, you do have feelings for me?"

"Yes. Of course. You know I do."

"But you don't want your mother to know. I can't do that, Sofia. I can't live like that. Once upon a time I did, but not anymore."

Sophia, still wearing her coat, hat, and gloves, moved past

Lacie and perched on the edge of the sofa at the opposite end. "She knows now. She knows everything. You. College. Everything."

Lacie didn't speak.

"I told her I'm in love with you."

The older woman's mouth dropped. When she regained her composure, she managed only, "You did?"

Sofia nodded. She slid a little closer to Lacie, but still kept some distance between them. "I did."

"How... how did she take that?"

Sophia gave her a half smile. "Not bad. A little shock at the 'love' part." She made air quotes. "Probably about the same as you are."

Lacie stood and pulled Sophia up. "Probably not. I love you too," she said, before capturing Sophia's lips in a kiss.

23

KENDALL CONNECTION

"Dad, I'm so sorry," Sophia told her father over her cell phone. "Slight change in plans. I won't be able to help with the feed inventory."

"Something wrong?"

"I'm with Lacie."

"I see."

His tone made her blush. "It's not... We've had a talk and now we're going to meet up with one of her coworkers... her friend and her... for brunch. Her best friend and her wife."

When her father didn't respond right away, she rushed on. "Well, anyway, I had a talk with Mom. She can explain why I left the house. I promised her I'd be back to help you though."

"It's okay, Sofia. You enjoy your time with Lacie and her friends. I think the hands can figure out how to stack bags of feed without you and get a good count of everything."

"Can we... Can we talk later?"

"Of course. Always."

The smile in his voice made her feel better. "Thanks, Dad."

"Give my love to Lacie."

"Okay." *Wow. Okay.*

. . .

SOPHIA SAT BACK in her chair, sated. "I feel like I've been eating all day." *Two breakfasts, and all...*

Kendall smiled. "I'm glad you enjoyed it."

Lacie, who had been arguing some of the finer points of a television show Sophia had never seen with Chris, looked down at her own half full plate. "Guess I'm a little behind."

Rising, Kendall picked up her plate and utensils but said to her friend, "There's no rush. Enjoy. I'm just going to put more coffee on and straighten up a little."

Sophia jumped to her feet and collected her own dishes. "Let me help you."

Kendall, hands full, tried to nod her back down. "It's fine. I've got it. Relax. Enjoy."

Sophia shot her a look that Kendall quickly picked up on. "But, if you'd like to keep me company for a few minutes?"

"Sure. Sure."

IN THE KITCHEN, after setting her dishes on the counter where Kendall had indicated, Sophia opted to come clean, quickly. "Lacie and I are seeing each other, we're together now."

Kendall laughed softly. "So I gathered."

"But, we weren't the night of the party."

"Sophia, you don't need to explain." She started rinsing the dishes they'd carried in.

"I do. It's literally just this morning that it's official." She took a deep breath. "I'm new at this. I came out to my mother just this morning. Less than two hours ago."

"Oh, sweetie!" Kendall dried her hands on a dish towel and enveloped Sofia in a hug.

After a few moments, they separated. "Can I ask, is Lacie your first?"

Sofia shook her head. "No. First in a while, but not my first. And, for what it's worth, my mom said she knew all along and she'd figured Lacie out. But..."

When her pause continued, Kendall prompted, "But you're worried about your mother's thinking on the whole thing?"

"Somewhat. But I'm even more worried about Lacie. We're so... so different and she's so much older than me."

"Let me tell you something, okay?"

Sophia gave her a nod.

Kendall leaned back against the counter. "I've known Lacie a long time. Since junior year at college. A long, long time ago–back then–we dated for about two minutes. A few days, tops. She never wanted to be tied down then and she didn't for years. Until now. Until you."

"You're sure?"

Kendall nodded. "She's the happiest I've ever seen her."

Sofia blew out a breath and said, "I'm not good at any of this. I don't have the experience she has. I'm worried I can't... can't keep her happy."

"Honey, how much do you know about Lacie?"

"Some. Not a lot. We spend most of our time together at the center. It's not really a good place to get to know someone. Not to get to know them romantically, anyway. I know she grew up in Oklahoma. She came here for school and stayed. She says it's more welcoming here."

Kendall nodded again as she reached out and took hold of one of Sofia's hands. "All of that is true, but I'm going to tell you something I probably shouldn't."

They heard laughter coming from the dining area. The sound of Lacie's laugh made Sofia smile. Kendall gave her a light elbow tap. "Girl, you got it bad."

Sofia didn't hesitate. "I do. I know. There's something about her. There's so much more than just what's on the surface."

"And that's part of what I was about to say. It took me years to get just a little information out of her. From what I gather, her childhood wasn't bad in some senses, but it was hard; if you know what I mean."

"Like the kids I work with?"

"Something like that, yes. Lacie's father left her mother when she was very young. Never looked back. She grew up with her mother and her grandmother, but not her mother's mom. Her father's mom. He had no contact with them, but they lived with her."

Sophia winced. "That must have been awkward for her mother."

"To say the least."

"And where are they now? Are they—"

"Still alive? Yes. Though I think her grandmother is up there in years. Lacie's father was several years older than her mother."

It all comes full circle.

"Has she... Does she go back to see them?"

Kendall shook her head. "Not that I'm aware of. She mentions them from time to time, so I know there's some sort of contact, but I don't know more than that, sorry."

I can't imagine not seeing my family for years on end. How does she do it?

LACIE GUIDED the car with her left hand while she held Sofia's hand loosely in her right hand. She stroked her thumb along the back of Sofia's fingers.

Sofia enjoyed the contact, but she couldn't relax. The thought of Lacie being estranged from all of her family ate at her. *I want to talk to her about it, but I don't know how to.*

"What's wrong?" Lacie asked.

"What? Nothing." She gave her what she hoped was a bright smile.

Lacie glanced over at her and caught the pasted-on grin, then lifted their linked hands. "You just tensed up."

"Oh. Sorry." She was silent for several beats.

"No secrets, okay? If there's something you want to know, just ask."

"What makes you think there's something I want to know?"

"Because you've been pensive ever since you came out of the kitchen with Kendall."

"You noticed, huh?"

"I notice everything."

Déjà vu.

"Did Kendall give you a hard time? I mean, it would surprise me because that's not her style, but if she did, I'd like to know about it."

Sofia pulled her hand away but turned slightly to face her lover. "Kendall's great. Chris too. You have some really great friends, and they care a lot about you."

"And I care about them."

She turned back, leaned her head back into the headrest, and closed her eyes. "What about your family, Lacie? I mean, you've mentioned growing up in Oklahoma. Is your family still there?"

"Yes. Well, some. There was never much of a clan to speak of. I have a grandmother there who's up there in years. Eighty-five. She's in a long-term care facility. My mom is back there as well."

"That's it?" She caught Lacie's nod as she opened her eyes. "No brothers or sisters? Aunts or uncles? Cousins? Nobody?"

"My mother left the tribe to marry my father. She was young and very pregnant. When she left, as she tells it, they turned their backs on her. I've never met any of her family at all."

Unreal. "Wow. I'm so sorry."

Lacie reached for her hand again and gave it a squeeze. "It's not your fault."

"Have you ever tried to find them?"

"No."

The way she said the word gave Sophia pause. "But you want to, don't you?"

"Someday. Maybe. She'd forbid it and I don't want to go behind her back to try."

"So, you're still in touch with her, then?"

Lacie simply nodded.

"Have you seen her?"

"It's been a long time. It was when we moved Gran to the nursing home about six years ago now. That's the last time I saw her. I was more focused on Gran then, but she didn't even know who I was anymore. Alzheimer's."

24

PARTY TIME!

Christmas Eve
Sun Valley Community Recreation Center
Denver, Colorado

L acie looked across the room when she caught a glimpse of the front door swinging open. She suppressed a sigh. It was just Will, followed by Ted and a crew from Tech Success with another load of gifts to tote in and stash for later, for after the children and their families had arrived.

She jumped when a hand touched her shoulder. Turning, she found a smiling Sophia.

"Where did you come from?"

"The alley. We have dad's truck back there to save a spot upfront for someone else to use. Besides, Mom had some last-minute stuff to bring."

Lacie looked her girlfriend up and down, taking in her red velvet form-fitting dress. "You look amazing."

Sophia preened at the compliment. "You like it?"

"I do." *I could eat you up right here. It's been way too long.* She tried to push her lust aside. "How did your last final go?"

"Good. I think I did well. The grades won't post until January 3rd, though."

Lacie leaned in a little closer. "I've missed you, what with your finals and all of this." She waved a hand about the room. "I really want to spend some time with you."

Hector Vaca cleared his throat.

Lacie spun and noticed both he and his wife had approached. *How do people keep sneaking up on me from behind?* "Mr. and Mrs. Vaca, uh..." she stammered. "Nice to see you."

"Hector, please. Call me Hector."

Judge Hildalgo joined Lacie and Will where they stood out of the way watching his wife, the Vaca women, and Brittney make short work of setting the food up just so on the buffet serving tables. "You two are doing what I always do," he said. "I stay out of their way." He turned to Will. "Good to see you again. Is your wife joining us tonight?"

"Likewise, Judge, and yes. She should be here any minute."

The judge then looked at Lacie. "And how are you getting along here?"

"Just fine, Judge. And, it's good to see you in..." she trailed off, unsure what to say. A blush stained her cheeks.

"She's too modest," Will said, saving her from sticking her foot in her mouth. "She's done some amazing work for us and gotten her company involved too." He tipped his head toward the far corner of the multi-purpose room floor. "That build-out over there? That's going to be our new computer lab and learning center."

Hildalgo raised an eyebrow. "Is that so?"

"I can't take all the credit," Lacie said. "There's a lot of sweat equity by Will and a couple of guys at my company to make that happen."

"But," Will interrupted, "you suggested the project, you did the assessment, and you got the funding and the manpower to make it happen. Credit where credit is due."

Lacie dipped her head in acknowledgement.

"Why don't you show him around, Lacie?" Will suggested. "I'm going to call my wife and see how close she is to getting here. The kids and their families will be coming soon."

"How many computers?" the judge asked Lacie.

"They've wired for ten. The building needed an electrical box upgrade. That was taken care of last week. This week they ran all the conduits into the lab room and started setting the grid up for the network, computers, printers and so forth. We'll wait to start putting up the drywall until after Christmas, when the center is closed for a week because that'll be a mess."

"You may not know this," Hildalgo said as they stepped inside the still empty framework of the future computer lab, "but Will has been sending me your hours. I was concerned you might not get all your time in before the end of the year. You've done what I hoped you would do here and that changes things in my estimation."

"Pardon? What did you hope I would do, Judge?"

"Exactly what you've done. Exactly what everyone does who comes into contact with Sun Valley. You gave it your heart."

Lacie smiled. "More than you know."

"Oh, if I were a betting man, I'd say I know more than you think I do."

"I'm sorry, Judge. I didn't mean—"

He waved her off. As he stepped back through the metal

framing for the door into the multi-purpose room, he looked back at her and said, "As for me, I'm really going to miss this place."

Stopping in the doorway, she gave him a quizzical look.

"I'm retiring. Thirty years on the bench is far more than enough. I've been trying to clear my docket, my cases. There's a primary in February. Some poor sap from the bar association has already thrown his hat in. I'm sure there will be others. I'll be replaced in June."

"Are you staying in the area?"

"For a time. We'll put our ranch up for sale. My wife is already in the process of selling off her catering business to two of her employees. They'll run it well."

"If you don't mind me asking, where will you go? Florida?"

"Heavens, no. Crazy political climate there and far too many retirees. We've already got a winter home in Ed Couch, Texas. We head there every year, right after Christmas, and stay until it's late spring here. Of course, I can only do a few days here and there, what with the court schedule and all, but my wife loves it." He smiled broadly. "Now we'll finally both be able to live in the sun and relax."

As they walked back toward the buffet set up, he told her, "Our ranch is just a small hobby venture. Forty acres. Horses are all we have. If you know anyone interested in something like that, or anyone looking for some property, let me know."

Lacie's mind whirred. "What about Hector and Eva?" *They'd be perfect. Finally have something to call their own.*

The judge laughed. "Don't think I didn't think of Hector first, but he says he's happy where he is. Eva too."

CLEVON JOGGED through the curtains beside the lighted, twinkling house they'd carefully removed from the trailer they'd used for the parade. His red and white track suit gave him a festive look. The Santa hat Sophia had convinced all the kids to wear for the show completed his ensemble.

"Welcome to Sun Valley Community Recreation Center! I'm Clevon Carry On. I'll be your host for this evening's festivities."

The crowd laughed.

Clevon feigned a backward lean. "Huh. That wasn't even a joke. Those come later!" More laughter rang out as the appreciative crowd settled in for the show.

"First up, we have our first and second graders who are going to sing you a little song I like to call 'wishful thinking.' We have Maya, James and Peaches singing 'Here Comes Santa Claus' for you."

The laughter from the crowd turned into coos about cuteness when the three youngest regulars filed out in Santa hats with elf ears and elf shoes.

Lacie beamed as she watched Brittney direct the little ones to the positions they'd practiced and then Sophia lead them in the song. She closed her mind to everything but what was going on right in front of her and clapped with the crowd when little Maya stepped forward and belted out her one-line solo with heartfelt aplomb, "So jump in bed and cover your head, cause Santa Claus comes tonight!"

"Isn't she the cutest thing?" Clevon asked the crowd as the standing ovation for the youngsters died down. "And those ears? They're all hers." The crowd chuckled. "You thought they were fake, didn't you? No, sir!" Everyone laughed again, then settled back in to see what was next.

Lacie and Sofia exchanged glances from ten feet apart, and Lacie flashed her girlfriend a thumbs up.

． ． ．

CLEVON WAS ON FIRE. "I don't know who Frosty disrespected more, me or my man, Will, over there."

Big laugh.

"And old Rudolph? He better watch going into sporting goods stores now! Seeing that is like when one of these kids sees Santa getting on the Broncos team bus after the parade."

Lacie glanced over and caught the eye of the Bronco's offensive line coach as he laughed along appreciatively. She nodded at him and mouthed 'thank you!' in his direction. At the request of the Tech Success CEO, he and a few of his players had shown up to work the crowd and one the children hadn't seen during the dinner service was all suited up to play Santa Claus as soon as Clevon took his final bow. *The boy doesn't know how close to the truth he is!*

Clevon cracked a couple of more one-liners, then took a half bow as the crowd clapped their appreciation.

"Thank you all so much," he continued more seriously as the room quieted down. "I'd like to bring everyone back out here one more time for a song." Brittney led all the children out from behind the makeshift curtains to stand in a line next to Clevon.

Whitney moved right up next to him, took his hand, and smiled up at him.

Sofia passed out dollar store candle shaped lights to the children while Will encouraged the members of the audience to turn on the candle lights they'd each been given after dinner. He went and stood behind the line of children.

It's all perfect, Lacie thought. With the small lights on, and all but a couple of the overhead gymnasium lights turned off, the big room took on a warm glow.

Will's deep baritone started 'Silent Night' with the children joining in at 'All is calm.' Soon, everyone in the room was singing.

As the last strains of the hymn drifted away, Clevon took a

half step forward and raised the Karaoke microphone back to his lips. "We'd like to thank you all for watching our show this evening and we wish everyone a very Merry Christmas. Please feel free to stay for cookies and punch and even an appearance by a very special guest."

On cue, sleigh bells rang out from outside the bay door to the back alley.

Maya jumped up and down. "Santa! It's Santa!"

"We'll see," Will called out as he rubbed his hands together in exaggerated glee as he left his place in their makeshift stage area and made his way to the wall switch that would allow him to raise the door.

The adults present laughed as a red Ford Bronco, driven by a Denver Broncos player pulled a flatbed trailer holding Santa's sleigh and a beaming Santa inside. The children missed the irony entirely, so spellbound were they by the mounds of gifts on the trailer and in the sleigh.

"I'M glad you could make it by, Jim," Lacie said to the Vice President of technology she'd been dreaming of replacing.

"You've done good work here, Lacie, circumstances aside. Very good work."

"Thank you."

"I had to come and see it for myself and let you in on something that was decided today." His tone grew more serious as he finished his sentence.

Lacie braced herself. "Oh. What's that?"

"We've made a decision on my replacement." His face gave nothing away. "We've decided to offer you the job."

Lacie caught sight of Sophia moving across the room toward them. She smiled more at her than at what she was hearing.

Jim went on. "There will be a more formal offer after the first of the year, of course. You'll want to put those analyst skills to use and figure out how much salary you're going to charge us." His laugh sounded a little rough to Lacie on his last point.

"How long do I have to decide?" she asked him.

"Pardon?"

"When do I need to give a decision?" she reiterated.

"On the salary?"

"No. On the position."

"I guess I didn't realize it was a question."

Because I'm just realizing that myself. "I don't mean to sound wishy-washy about it, Jim. Can you give me until the 26th to say for sure before you have the board put a formal offer together? I need to think through a couple of things, is all. It won't take long."

He looked her over critically before he gave in. "I suppose. The 26th though, no later. There were other viable candidates and I leave soon. We'll want someone in position quickly so I can show them the ropes, so to speak."

"Yes. Of course."

Jim dipped his head in acknowledgement when Sophia joined them. "Very nice party, Miss."

"Thank you so much, but I came over here to thank you. We couldn't have done it without you and Tech Success. I mean, just look at those kids. They're over the moon with their gifts. And, I've also just been informed there's a dinner box for every family for tomorrow on that flatbed, too. That's so amazing and generous."

He cracked a slight smile. "I can't take all the credit, or even any of it, for that matter. It was all Lacie's doing and the company's willingness to open the checkbook."

"I'm going to hug you anyway, on behalf of the center, in thanks to Tech Success."

Lacie looked on, wishing it was her Sophia hugged with her

soft curves as Jim stood his ground and accepted her heartfelt thank you with more than a little of what Lacie read as embarrassment on his face. *I never did see him as the huggable type.*

After he extricated and excused himself, Sophia focused on Lacie. "I wasn't sure I should come over here. The two of you looked like you were having an intense conversation."

"He offered me the VP job; the one he's retiring from."

"Oh, wow! That's great!"

"Yeah."

She was saved by saying more when Eva and Brittney approached them.

Eva said, "Sofia, it looks like we're about done with the food cleanup here."

Sophia didn't have time to answer before Britt put in, "I think this was the best party here, ever."

"Yes," Sophia said. "The kids had a great time...and the gifts. Wow!"

Eva threw up a hand. "Even without all the hullabaloo, you did a great job. All of you. Something to be proud of, the way everyone gave back tonight."

"Thank you, Mom."

Lacie, taking a contrite stance with her hands clasped in front of her, said, "Thank you from me to you as well. You haven't stopped moving all night."

Eva brushed the implied compliment off, saying, "I sort of pushed to get all the serving done and all of that cleaned up. We ran a little later this year than last year, and I'd like to run home and change clothes before Midnight Mass." She looked at Sophia and Britt, and then at Lacie. "You're all welcome to join me there."

Brittney begged off. "Frank is picking me up here shortly and we're going over to his brother's house."

Lacie glanced at Sofia. "I'll go if you want. I've never been to a Catholic Christmas Eve service." *As long as the floor doesn't open up and swallow us whole, it can't be that bad.*

Sofia looked at her watch and declined for both of them. "Lacie and I promised to be out and about early in the morning picking up kids to bring them out to the ranch. It's after 9:30, now. There's still clean up to do and some other loose ends to wrap up."

25

I'LL BUY YOU A TOASTER OVEN

Late Christmas Eve
Lacie's Condo
Denver, Colorado

L acie collapsed onto her sofa next to Sofia. "I'm exhausted. I don't know how you younger people do it."

"Stop!" Sophia cautioned her. "You're not *that* old."

"I know. It's just been a long day, I guess. A long one, but a good one."

"Yes. Thank you for that."

"It wasn't all me. Everyone keeps trying to give me so much credit that I don't deserve." She sighed. "After all, remember why I'm even helping at the center in the first place."

"You've come a long way from that in about six weeks, Lacie."

That's kind of what the judge said, too. "I guess. I just feel like there's so much more I could do."

"You've done a lot."

"No. My company has done a lot."

"At your insistence." When Lacie didn't answer, she went on. "None of that would have happened without you in there pushing for it."

Lacie leaned in a little closer, her lips inches from Sophia's. "I don't want to fight." She brushed Sophia's lips with a soft kiss. Her overture became passionate quickly. She deepened the kiss when she felt the younger woman melt against her.

When they finally parted, Sophia shook her head. "Thought you were tired?"

"I am, but I've missed you."

"We've seen each other almost every day."

"Yeah. Publicly. A quick, stolen kiss here and there. No proper dates or anything like that."

Sophia gave in. "I've regretted not having time, just us, too." She moved away and sank back into the cushions of the sofa. "It's not really going to get any easier, is it? I'll have grad school. You'll have your new job. We'll both be pretty busy."

Lacie drew in a deep breath. "There's a solution." *Can't believe I'm about to say this.* She let the breath out in a rush and blurted, "Move in with me." *Can't believe I said it.* "You'd be closer to campus and to the center. We could see each other every day; be together every night—"

"That sounds tempting, but you're forgetting something."

"What? Your mother?" She caught a flicker of something pass through her lover's eyes. "I'm sorry." She held out a hand. "I didn't mean to upset you."

Sofia sucked in a deep breath of her own and held it for a few seconds before letting it out slowly.

"Counting to ten?"

"Relaxation breathing, but both techniques work." She

accepted the offered hand and held Lacie's as she spoke. "I love you."

"I love you too."

"I'm a big girl. I need to be strong enough to deal with my mother's misgivings on my own. That's my hang-up to get over, not my mom's. Not yours. My issue is, aside from how I feel about you, we don't really know each other that well yet. And," she went on when Lacie started to lean in and say something, "I still have a job at the ranch, and I need it. There's no guarantee what the funding will be like for the center. No guarantee if I'll be paid. If I were to stay here," she waved her free hand about, "it will be tough for me to get down there during the hours they need me."

"Hear me out, okay?"

"Okay."

Lacie felt her response was tentative, so she chose her words carefully. "They offered me the VP of technology job, like I told you earlier. I can pretty much write my own ticket. I'm already comfortable. I own this place outright. I have more than enough, and I want to share that with you."

Sofia shook her head. "Lacie, stop. There's no way I can take your money."

"It would be *our* money. I'll put you on all of my accounts." *Never thought I'd ever say that to anyone.*

"Wow. Okay." She blinked her eyes a couple of times. "While I appreciate what you're trying to do here, you don't understand where I'm coming from. Grad school is expensive, even at City. My parents helped with my BA, and I got scholarships. I can't ask them to pay for grad school. I won't. And, I certainly won't ask you to pay for it. I've saved some money away, enough for nearly the first year. I planned to keep working and scrimp for the rest; only use loans as a last resort."

Lacie pressed her. "I know you love the horses, but this

could be so good for us. I'll earn a lot more. If we're together, you won't have to work your way through your master's program at the ranch or worry about the center's finances. You can stay there, at the center, doing what you love, no matter what."

Sophia dropped Lacie's hand. "I don't want to fight about this with you. Even though I'd love to spend every free minute here with you... even though I want to be with you, I never want to feel like I'm not carrying my own weight. I know I would feel like that for sure if I was living here, not working for pay, and you were paying my tuition."

Lacie leaned her head back into the cushions and let out a heavy breath. "I get that, I guess."

"Can I ask you something?"

"Of course. No secrets, remember?"

"Nothing like that. It's just... this new job. You don't seem as excited about it as you were when you first told me about it back at the sandwich shop, even with using it to get me to move in now that it's been offered to you. Is that job what you really want, after all?"

"I've worked for it for so long. I really want to move on from there with Tech Success, or even somewhere else and be their senior technology person or their CTO." *Or, at least, I did.*

"We've only known each other about six weeks, is all, but I think I can tell when you're excited about something and when you're not."

"I'm excited about having a future with you, even though it's *only* been six weeks."

"And I get that. I want that too." She gave Lacie a soft smile. "Let's drop it for now. We can talk more after Christmas."

I need to make a decision soon. I guess I have some choices to make. She smiled back at her girlfriend. "It's a date. Now, if you're really planning on staying the night, we should get to bed... if any sleep at all is in our future plans." She tried to raise her eyebrows suggestively, but she elicited laughter.

"You're tired, remember?"

"Honey, I'm never too tired to make love to you."

"Oh." Sofia blushed.

As for the rest, I may have to make a choice. I'm starting to feel like my career with Tech Success isn't as important to me as it once was. Certainly not as important as this raven-haired beauty I want to keep by my side forever.

LACIE WRAPPED an arm around Sofia and pulled her in tight. The younger woman's soft curves felt like silk to her.

She nibbled at the tender skin of Sofia's neck, starting behind her ear, then moving down her throat to the curve of her shoulder.

Sofia arched and sighed.

She licked her fingers and stroked them over Sofia's nipples, tormenting and torturing them until Sofia put a fist to her mouth and bit down to silence a scream.

Lacie stopped what she was doing and pulled the fist away.

"Your neighbors! They'll hear me."

"So? *I* want to hear you. I want you to tell me what you want."

Arching up again, Sofia stretched for Lacie's lips and pressed a hungry kiss to them.

Lacie's hands caressed lower down Sophia's stomach. She touched her everywhere, feeling her body warm under her palms. Her thighs fell open. Lacie lifted one to rest atop her legs and eased a knee in between. She flexed her muscles and teased Sofia's drenched center with pressure from her leg.

Backing off after several long seconds just a bit with her knee, she snaked in with a hand as Sofia writhed from the missing contact. She dipped her fingers into her core and caressed her. Sofia tightened on her fingers. *She's close.*

Sofia bucked. Her body was shaking. "Lacie!" she called out.

No muffling it this time! Lacie quickened the pace with her thigh and her fingers.

Sophia gasped, coming.

Lacie didn't quit until she settled. When she finally slipped her fingers from her lover's pussy, Sofia surprised her by grabbing the hand and rolling them.

"My turn!"

26

MISFIT CHRISTMAS

Christmas Morning
Greenfield Village

Sophia stretched out against Lacie who spooned her, naked, from behind. The older woman's body gave her comfort as some time in the night, the fireplace had been turned off, leaving them with only the central heating of the condo and Lacie's body heat. Lacie's comforter and silk sheets lay in tangles along the footboard and on the floor.

Lacie must have felt her move. She splayed a hand across Sofia's stomach and pulled her in tighter to her pelvis.

Fully awake then, Sophia's core came alive. She felt her wetness from the night before returning and she tried to stifle a moan. She didn't fool Lacie.

Lacie half sat up, grabbed at the comforter, and yanked it up over them as she lay back down. She returned her hand to its former position, making sure Sofia was tucked into her tight, then hooked it under her left thigh and lifted her left leg up over her own. She wasted no time reaching back around her lover and finding her clit with her traveling hand.

Moments later, the first wave of Sophia's orgasm washed over her. She writhed about, but Lacie held her firmly back.

"Oh, what you do to me," she panted out later as she tried to catch her breath. "I don't know how much more of that I can—"

"There's a lot more. A whole lot," Lacie said, before claiming her lips in a kiss.

"We've got to go!"

Lacie grinned. "If you hadn't kept us in bed so long, we—"

"Me? You're the one who...!"

Lacie laughed as she pulled Sofia into a hug. "I love you."

"I love you too," Sofia said as she pulled away. "Now really, let's go. We've got to get Maya first and then Clevon and his grandma."

"Maya's mom isn't coming?" Lacie shot the question back over her shoulder as she stepped into the garage and pushed the button to open the bay door.

Sofia started to answer but had to draw up short to keep from running into Lacie.

"Whoa!" Lacie said. She turned halfway around, allowing Sofia room to move past her as she asked, "Did you look outside at all this morning?"

"Um, no. I was sort of in a rush." Sofia looked toward the open bay door. "Oh. Okay. It looks like about six inches."

"And about five and a half more than the dusting of snow they were calling for us to get overnight."

Sophia spread her hands. "We'll have that. Merry Christmas, Colorado."

"My Subaru can handle it, but I don't know about horseback riding in this."

As she moved on by her girlfriend, Sophia chuckled. "This is nothing the horses can't handle. The sky is clear, and the sun is coming up. We'll be fine." She yanked open the passenger door to Lacie's car and called out as she climbed in, "Let's go!"

～

"OH, what a lovely home, and it smells heavenly in here," Clevon's grandmother, Elizabeth, exclaimed as she, Sofia, Lacie, and the kids crossed the threshold into the living room.

"Merry Christmas and welcome," Eva said, "and thank you. We're having ham and all the trimmings later. You're all staying, I hope?"

"Of course they are," Hector said as he clapped Clevon on the shoulder. "We're hoping to have some fresh catch to gut and try out too."

Clevon's eyes grew large. "Gut?"

"Yes. Fish are just like any animal, you know. There's a process."

The teenager swallowed hard.

"Come on, son," Hector told him. "Let's get you outfitted to go. I've got a hut, but you're still going to need to bundle up some more."

"Hut?"

"A fishing hut," Sofia explained to him. "You'll be out on a frozen lake. There's lots of wind so it can be pretty cold if you don't have a hut."

"Uh, Mr. Vaca, no offense," Clevon plead, "but maybe we should do this in the summer when it's warmer. A *lot* warmer."

Sofia and Lacie laughed, but Hector and Gramma Elizabeth both spoke to Clevon at once. "You'll be fine, you'll see," Elizabeth said. "You're going to love it just like your pap did."

Hector told him, "You won't even notice the cold once we get going, and I'm going to get you dressed as warm as possible before we step out the door."

Maya moved over and tugged Sofia's hand. "What about me on the horse? Won't I be cold?"

After giving the small hand a squeeze, Sofia promised, "No way! We're going to have a great time. You'll see."

Maya smiled and looked at Clevon's grandmother. "Are you going fishing with them, or riding with me?"

"Oh, child. These old bones don't do well in the cold. I'd like to see all of it, but with all the snow we got out there last night—"

"We can see the paddock where they'll start out with Maya, right from the breakfast nook window, Elizabeth," Eva said. "And later, if you want, we can take a ride over to the lake and check on the other two. We can take them some fresh hot chocolate."

Clevon smiled at that. "You'll come see me, won't you, Gramma?"

"It's not too bad, Elizabeth," Hector said. "My hut isn't far from the edge of the lake and your boots look like they'll do you fine. It's supposed to be sunny today. "

"Okay then." She wagged a finger at her grandson. "You do what Hector tells you. Follow directions. The water under that ice will be crazy cold and you can't swim."

The teenager nodded.

"And you be sure to catch some fish for me to see when I come over there."

"Yes, ma'am."

Lacie

After watching Sofia lead Maya off somewhere else in the house in search of snow pants that had been left behind by one of the Vaca grandchildren, and after pointing out the bathroom to Elizabeth, Lacie let realized she was alone in the living room with Eva. *Play it cool. You kept her daughter out all night on Christmas Eve. She's got to be mad.*

She smiled at the elder Vaca woman. "It really does smell wonderful in here."

"There was ham last night at the party," Eva pointed out.

"And turkey. I ate the turkey."

"We... Hector and I, at least, still follow the traditional Catholic fasting rules and we don't eat meat on Christmas Eve."

"Oh. I hadn't realized."

"Sofia does. Eat meat on Christmas Eve, I mean."

I thought I saw ham on her plate!

"Sofia's doing a lot of things differently these days."

Oh boy. "Listen, I'm sorry about last night. I really am. First, we broke down the cookies and parceled them out to a lot of the families that hung around to help take down the tables and chairs. Not many of the goodies got eaten once Santa showed up. Then, it was nearly eleven when we finished cleaning up."

"It's okay," Eva said, waving off any further explanation. "You don't owe me a reason. Sofia is an adult. She can make her own decisions, and I can learn to deal with that thought. I will learn to deal with that." Her voice was firm. Confident.

Not knowing what else to do or say, Lacie gave her a slight nod.

"She loves you, Lacie." The words came in a softer tone.

Lacie didn't waste time responding with, "And I love her."

Eva nodded, then. "I only ask one thing. You go at her pace, please. You haven't known each other that long."

Lacie drew in a breath and tried to steady herself. "I asked her to move in with me last night. She said no."

Eva moved from the entry area where they were still standing and sat down on the edge of an armchair. "I appreciate you admitting that. Did she say no because of me?"

Lacie moved around the end of the sofa and sat, too. "No. It's not really for me to go into, but I will say that her heart is in the right place."

"It's school, isn't it?"

"That's part of it, yes."

"Money." Eva's tone was matter of fact.

"Yes. That too. Work, more specifically." *And I feel like a heel giving up her confidences so easily.* "I can help her... want to help her, but she's very independent." *At least, she is in that regard.*

"She's always been a giver, Lacie. Never a taker. I don't expect that will change."

Elizabeth rejoined them, cutting their conversation short. Lacie tried to stifle her sigh of relief.

"It's a little colder out here than we thought," Lacie said to Sofia as Sofia and Maya passed the paddock fence rail she was leaning on. The horse Sofia led didn't seem to mind the cold though, and its young rider also seemed oblivious.

"She's loving it, aren't you, Maya?" Sofia asked her as they halted their progress.

Maya's voice rang with enthusiasm. "Yes! Can we go further? You let go and let me ride him?"

"Her. Shannon's a mare, remember sweetie, and no. You're not quite ready for that yet, but you can ride with me on a trail ride, and I'll let you help guide the reins. How about that?"

Maya's initial pouty face turned into a smile. "Sure. Let's go."

Sofia laughed. "Not so fast. We have to pick a horse for Lacie and get it saddled up, first."

"Oh boy," Lacie said. "I can hardly wait."

"It's a working ranch," Sofia reminded her when she caught the hesitation in her tone. As she looped Shannon's reins around the rail, she went on, "There are lots of well-trained horses here. You'll be fine."

"It's just, it's been a long time. How about I take that Shannon? She seems gentle, easygoing. I'll help you saddle up another one for you."

"I suppose. I mean, Shannon's technically my horse, and I was going to ride with Maya on her too."

"Oh. Is there another horse like her, then?"

Sofia tapped her lip with a gloved finger and thought for a minute. "Chet. He's the foreman's backup now that he has a new ride. He's halfway to retirement and an all-around great horse."

"One hoof in the glue factory. Sounds perfect!"

"Glue factory?" Maya questioned.

Sofia shot Lacie a look. "We don't do that here!"

27

FULL CIRCLE

"Where are we going?" Lacie asked, as they halted the horses at the edge of I-85 while they waited for traffic to pass. They were less than a mile from the ranch.

Sofia pointed across the street. "That forested area over there is a part of Chatfield State Park. There are lots of easy horse trails... and a surprise."

Maya let out a little squeal from in front of Sofia. "A surprise?"

"Yes."

"What is it?"

"It wouldn't be a surprise if I told you, would it?"

Lacie eyed Sofia as they began to cross side by side. Her face gave nothing away. "A good surprise, I hope."

Sophia's tone suggested a smirk. "Aren't all surprises good?"

"No. No, they're not."

"Well, I think they are. I love them," Maya said.

They rode on a trail, one behind the other through the leafless park trees for several minutes with Sophia letting Maya take the reins for a long stretch.

The sun was out, shining through the bare branches, warming them as they passed along. Though bare, the trees had shielded the trail from some of the snow, and the sun was taking care of much of the rest of what managed to accumulate. Still, Lacie could hear the horse's hoofs crunch along as they picked their way along the path.

"I'll bet this was pretty when the leaves were turning," Lacie said.

Sophia looked back over her shoulder, smiling. "It's pretty now, too. Actually, this is one of my favorite places to ride in every season. I just don't get to do it much anymore."

The trail widened, so Lacie drew alongside Sofia and Maya. "The owner lets you take Shannon out, just to ride?"

"She's not working ranch stock; she's breeding stock. She has to be exercised, so yes."

"Breeding means she makes babies," Maya informed them.

Lacie coughed and sputtered, but Sophia took the child's pronouncement in stride. "That's what it means, yes. We get new horses to raise for the ranch all the time from horses like Shannon."

The trail started to narrow. Lacie slowed Chet down, intending to fall behind again, but Sophia waved her forward. "You lead for a while. Take the next trail that opens to the left."

Half an hour and a couple more left turns later, Lacie realized, though they were on a different northward trail, they had made a complete loop. She pulled back on the reins and commanded Chet to halt.

Sophia and Maya stopped alongside her.

Lacie asked, "What's going on? We're going in circles."

"Just giving Maya more of a ride... and killing a little bit of time."

"Well," Lacie began in a whisper, "My butt hurts."

Maya laughed, making Lacie grimace all the more.

Sophia said, "That's because you've been bouncing a bit in the saddle. You're not in rhythm, yet."

"I told you, it's been a long time. How much further until we get—" She dropped the reins with one hand and threw it up in the air. "I don't even know where we're going."

"To the surprise," Maya put in.

Sofia gave the six-year-old a quick hug from behind. "That's right, and it's just up ahead. Are you ready to see it?"

"Yeah!" Lacie and Maya answered in unison.

Sophia took control of the reins and commanded Shannon forward with the cluck of her tongue and a little pressure from her heels.

After a few minutes, the trail began to widen. Soon, they came out of the trees into the wide-open spaces leading down to a large, frozen lake. The parking lot a short distance ahead of them and to their right was about a quarter full of pickup trucks.

Out on the lake, snowmobiles and ATVs were dotted here and there among ice fishing shacks that extended from about fifty yards off the shore to a few hundred yards out.

"What is this?" Maya asked.

"I think this is probably where Mr. Vaca and Clevon are, Maya," Lacie answered.

Sofia said, "She's right."

"Oh! Can we go see if they caught anything? Can we?" The girl bounced in the saddle with her excitement. Shannon stood still and took it like she was used to having such a young, exuberant rider.

More for Lacie than Maya, Sofia said, "That's why we were circling around. I was giving them time to get here, get settled in and hopefully catch a few."

Maya pointed at the lake. "Which one of those is your dad's fishing house?"

"Hut. It's called a hut. Let's go tie up the horses and I'll let you try to guess while we walk out to it."

Maya turned in the saddle and shot her a pouty faced look. "Why can't we ride the horses out there?"

"Oh, no." Sophia cautioned. "It's too dangerous for them."

"Okay, wait a minute," Lacie began. "We can walk out there, but they can't? People have snowmobiles and quads out there too."

"Trust me," Sophia said. "It's too slippery for the horses. We don't want any broken legs?"

Lacie muttered something about her own legs, but Sofia ignored her.

IN THE PARKING LOT, a sense of déjà vu overcame Lacie. She tried to stifle a shudder, but Sofia noticed.

"Cold?"

Lost in her thoughts, the question caught her off guard. "Huh?"

"Are you cold?"

"No. No. I uh... I was just thinking." She looked around from atop Chet, trying to get her bearings.

Sofia finished tying off the horses at the rail and helped Maya down. She turned back to Lacie. "Are you coming?"

"Yeah. Sure." She dismounted and fell in beside Sofia.

"You look like you saw a ghost."

"I may have."

"Where?" Maya asked. She pointed at the lake. "Out there, where we're going?"

"It's just an expression," Sophia explained.

"But she said she may have seen a ghost. Ghosts are scary."

"What I meant to say was, I think I've been here before, but I'm not sure," Lacie said.

Sophia shot her a look. "It happened here?"

"I think so. I mean, it was summer, and it was nearly dark when we got here. It was very dark when... when we left. This parking lot though and the railing where you just tied us off... I remember hanging onto the railing while—"

Maya tugged at Sophia's hand and interrupted. "Come on! Let's go." She pointed toward the huts. "I think it's that pretty blue one out there."

They started walking that way. "No. It's not blue," Sophia told her. "And it's not that far out. It's pretty close to the shore."

"Shore?"

"Where the land meets the lake," Lacie explained.

Maya said, "I've never been to a lake before."

I'm not surprised. "Really? Well, we'll just have to bring you back in the summer when the water is all thawed out. We can swim."

Sofia gave Lacie a big grin. "Bad feelings are already gone, eh?"

Lacie shrugged, but Sofia missed it because Maya was bubbling over again. "I ain't never been swimming either. Can Shannon come? Do horses know how to swim?" Before anyone could answer, she pointed to another hut, this time a little closer. "How about that one with the shiny roof?"

"Nope. Not that one," Sophia said, "but you're getting closer."

They picked their way down the shore toward a hut with muted red siding and a shingled roof.

Maya tried to skip when she saw which hut they were angling toward, but Sofia held her back. "This is snow and sand right here, but we're going to be on ice in a few seconds, and—"

"Hello, there!" came a call from behind them.

"Mom?" Sofia whirled and almost fell herself. Behind them, having just started down the beach from the parking lot were her mother and Clevon's grandmother.

As she looked back too, Lacie said, "The more the merrier, I guess."

"It was going to be crowded in there with the three of us and the two of them. I didn't expect they'd be out here so soon," Sofia answered.

Maya gave a little hop. "Let's go. We can go first and then take turns in there."

"How about I go back and help your mom get Gramma Elizabeth down here?" Lacie said to Sophia. "You can let Maya in to get a decent look."

"Good plan, but I want you to see this too."

"Looking forward to it."

"Is that sarcasm?"

"No. I really am looking forward to it." With that, she turned and headed back up the beach toward the older pair.

"I WAS NEVER in your pap's ice fishing hut," Gramma told Clevon after he showed her and Maya the one fish he'd caught to Hector's two. "Fishing was his reprieve from everything else, and I let him have it to himself." She took another look around the small hut. "Not bad. Not all of the creature comforts, but not bad. It's certainly warmer in here than I thought it would be."

Hector smiled. "You don't need much out here, Elizabeth. A couple of seats, a good saw, and somewhere to set your coffee so it's not sitting on the ice, getting cold. I'm not into all those iced espresso things."

Sofia poked her head around from outside the doorway. "Iced latte, Dad. Not espresso."

Lacie, who was standing outside with Sofia but square with the doorway so she could look inside, produced the thermos she'd carried down for Eva when she helped her escort Elizabeth onto the ice. "I've got your refill here." She passed it inside to Eva to pass on.

"Actually," Eva said from her position just inside the door, "This is hot chocolate for Clevon, like I promised."

Clevon clapped his gloved hands together. "Oh boy, am I ready for that." He peeled the gloves off and reached for the thermos, wrapping his hands around its warmth when Eva handed it over.

"Well, I have to say, this looks a lot safer than I pictured it being," Elizabeth said. "There are a lot of these huts out here. Don't hear anyone screaming for help or anything because they fell in."

Clevon let go of the Thermos with one hand and pointed at the hole in the ice their lines were in. "It would be hard to fall into that, Gramma."

"Ice breaks, boy, and you can't swim."

He responded through gritted teeth. "Why you gotta keep reminding me? It's embarrassing."

"The ice is six or seven inches thick here, Elizabeth," Hector said, "and I've got him. He's safe with me."

Maya ventured a little closer to the hole. "I can't swim either and I might fit in there."

Hector put out an arm and nudged her back. "Let's not test it."

Sofia stuck her head through the door and spoke to the teenager. "It's nothing to be ashamed of, Clevon, but it's something that's easy to fix. The Rude Rec Center is only a couple of blocks from us. They give free lessons in their pool year-round. We could get you hooked up over there, have you swimming by summer. You too, Maya."

"That's probably a bunch of little kids, though, right?"

"Probably, yes. But if you learn now, you could swim

anywhere. Don't you have friends that go to one of the city pools?"

"Yeah," he admitted.

"Or," Hector offered, "You could come out here once in a while, get out of the city. We might even be able to go fishing. I don't get a lot of time off in the summer, but this is a nice place to spend some of it when I do."

Clevon's eyes shone. "Can I, Gramma?"

"You listen to Mr. Vaca today and you take those lessons, then we'll see."

"Okay." His tone was resigned, but he perked up quickly when Hector pointed out the movement in his line.

"Come on Maya, that's our cue to leave and give them some room," Sofia called to the six-year-old.

～

Christmas Night
The Vaca Living Room

Lacie

LACIE SANK onto the sofa and sighed. "I ate too much and I'm tired. Ya'll wore me out again today."

"You've even reverted to southern speak," Sophia laughed.

Lacie lolled her head back and forth against the cushions. "I'm just going to sit a minute and then I'm going to head home, to my bed whom I'm sure appreciates me."

"I know you're joking, but I want you to know a lot of people appreciate you. You've done so much to help so many the past couple of months."

She gave her girlfriend a tired smile. "We've been over this. You don't have to keep thanking me. I really don't deserve it."

Sofia sat down on the edge of the sofa. "Let me ask you something. How did you feel today at the lake, when you realized where we were?"

"Weird."

"Weird, how?"

"I don't know. Nervous, I guess. Almost sick to my stomach."

"Why?"

Lacie shrugged. "Because... Because, you know. It's where I... where I got in trouble." She whispered the last part even though they were alone. Eva and Hector were out, taking Grandma and the kids back into Denver in exchange for Sophia and Lacie cleaning up the kitchen and the dinner dishes.

"When did that happen again?"

"When I got in trouble? July."

"So, six months ago."

Lacie nodded.

"You really weren't that person then, Lacie."

"I'm not sure what you mean."

"Were you ever in any kind of legal trouble before that?"

"No. I told you that."

"Right. That was a onetime thing."

"That will never happen again."

"Right. That whole night was out of character for you. Now, let me ask you this—"

"You're starting to sound like a social worker."

Sophia cracked a smile. "Continuing on, I was about to ask you, do you feel like you've changed at all since that time especially the last couple of months?"

"I'm not trying to be obtuse here. Really, I'm not, but

changed how? I mean, I fell in love. There's that..."

"So did I," Sophia admitted. "But you've really changed as a person, too. You've gone from being all business and just wanting to put in your time to bending over backwards to help the center and to help the kids."

Lacie blushed. "I guess I never thought about it that way." She started thinking about everything that had occurred in the time since she'd been summoned to Judge Hildalgo's office to hear her fate. "I didn't tell you, the judge says I've met my sentencing requirements."

"Oh." Sophia sat back.

"I'm not going anywhere, hon. I'm going to be there every step of the way with the computer lab build out, swimming lessons, you name it."

"You... you can't."

Lacie arched an eyebrow at her girlfriend. "Why not?"

"Your job, Lacie. You take enough time away now. Once you're in your new position—"

"I've thought about that all day. I'm not going to take the job."

"What? Why?"

"It's not for me." *It's really not.* "I guess you're right. I guess I have changed."

"So, you'll stay in your current position?"

"Yes, but not for long." She moved closer to Sophia and took her hand.

Sophia let her hold it, but she kept up the questions. "What will you do, instead?"

"Let's just say, a plan is starting to form."

She leaned in and kissed Sofia softly, but she didn't linger. Rising, she said to her, "Your mom and dad will be home soon, and I really am tired. Call me in the morning, or just come over if you can. You can help me make plans."

EPILOGUE: AKA 'WHAT HAPPENED TO THEM?'

Saturday, September 18th
Highlands Ranch, Colorado

Lacie finished saddling the mare and handed the reins off to Clevon. "Now remember, walk her around to the back of the barn and tie her off. We don't want Sofia to see her."

He pretended to tip a cowboy hat to her as he answered, "Gotcha, boss!"

"Ha ha. Very funny... not. Giving you a pay job might have been a mistake. I think I liked it better when you just called me Miss Lacie."

Will caught the last bit as he sauntered into the barn. "Good luck with ever going back in time now. Not with him."

"Hey now," Clevon said to Will as he led Lacie's horse by, "I resemble that remark."

Will shook his head. "Oh, that's good. Very good. You've turned one of my favorite sayings around on me."

Lacie suppressed her inclination to laugh. "Step it up, Clevon," she called after the teen instead. "Sophia will be here thinking she's going to conduct the riding session any minute now."

She spoke to Will as he approached her then. "I'm so glad you could make it down here."

"Are you kidding? I wouldn't have missed this!"

Hector walked into the barn and called out, "She just pulled in, driving the center van with all the kids. Everyone be cool!"

Lacie couldn't help herself. She had to laugh at that. Her ranch manager and do-gooder in chief was more nervous about her plan than she was. She shooed him back out. "Go out there with the horses. We don't want her to think anything is weird."

He tossed over his shoulder as he began to leave, "The judge wanted to leave his packing up chores for a minute and join us." He stopped and half turned back to her. "I didn't think you'd mind. He's hiding out on the back porch with Eva."

Lacie tried to hide her surprise that either the elder Vaca woman or the judge were taking an interest. *It's Sofia though. I should have figured.* "The more the merrier, now git!"

As Hector hustled out, Will asked, "Where do you want me?"

"I'm going around to the back to get on my horse. You peek out the door up there and come out when you see me ride by. The kids will key in on me, so she probably will too."

Lacie took a deep breath after she mounted her white Arabian mare, Lago Snow. *Here goes! Hope I gave them enough time.*

She trotted the horse easily around the barn, toward the riding paddock. She caught a glimpse of Will stepping out from behind the barn door and sat up tall in the saddle. She knew all eyes would be on her.

Don't screw this up, she told herself as she gave the mare a pat. She knew Lago would do her part. *Can't guarantee I won't fall off her out of sheer nervousness, though.*

The children were mounted on their horses as she and

Hector had planned with them. They began moving into the positions she'd marked out for them with subtle marks on the fencing as guides. They formed the shape of a heart with Sophia at the point.

Lacie smiled when she realized Sophia didn't seem to notice the sudden proficiency of her equine therapy charges to guide their horses without her commands. *I've got to credit Hector there with getting them positioned right and the right kid to the right horse to begin with.*

Hector must have read her thoughts. He dipped his head in acknowledgement.

Sophia stopped talking to the kids and looked out at her. Then she saw Will. She called to him, rather than to Lacie, "Will, what's going on?"

Eva and Judge Hildalgo, now retired, stepped off the judge's back porch and moved quickly toward the riding paddock while Clevon opened the gate for Lacie to ride through.

Lacie entered the paddock and rode Lago around the left side of the heart formation, stopping when she reached Sophia and her mount, Shannon, whom Lacie had purchased from the rancher the Vaca's had formerly worked for.

Clevon closed the gate behind himself, then walked through the center of the heart to meet her when she stopped. He took Lago's reins while Lacie began the speech she'd tried to practice, but could never get quite right, to her own satisfaction.

Lacie reached over and took Sophia's shaking hand. With her other hand, she pointed around at each member of the group. "It started with you, Clevon, me, Will, Whitney, Nelda, DeMarco, Maya, and with several others who are not here, but who have benefitted from the services of the Sun Valley Rec Center and from this place we now, with the blessing of Judge Hildalgo, call Misfit Ranch." She tipped her hat to the judge who had willingly sold her his property when he heard what she wanted to do with it.

"You've taught me so much, Sofia. How to always see the best in everyone and everything. How to make something from nothing. How to share what I have and watch it go ten times further. And you've taught me what love is. Real love. True love. For those reasons, and so many more, I want to spend every day of the rest of my life with you, learning, growing, and loving."

She let go of Sofia for a moment while she untied the bit of ribbon she'd looped around Lago's saddle horn and slid the band of turquoise encrusted with a single diamond off the rose-colored curl. She picked the hand back up, but she realized too late she was on the wrong side for what she'd intended.

Clevon looked up at her, eyes wide, as she dropped Sofia's right hand and reached for her left.

Sophia raised her quivering left hand to her mouth as tears began to form at the corners of her eyes.

"Sophia Vaca, would you marry me and be my partner in life, in love, and in ranching and reaching out to kids, for life?" She began to slide the ring on Sophia's finger before an answer even came.

Clevon nodded at Sophia. The other kids began to cheer and clap before she uttered a word in response.

Lacie held her breath. *Too soon? Am I being presumptuous? Oh, maybe I shouldn't have done this so publicly!*

Sofia looked at her father, standing at the fence near the gate and at her mother standing next to the judge around the side of the paddock fence and then, finally, back at Lacie. She glanced down at the ring, then back up into her eyes. "Yes. Yes. I will marry you."

AFTERWORD

Aside from pieces of the setting, this story is completely fictional. The city of Denver has an amazing network of community centers that provide an array of services to the entire population of the city. Many of those services are given free of charge or at very low cost to metro area residents, regardless of income or ability to pay.

The Sun Valley neighborhood is real. It's a small community in the orbit of the Denver downtown metro area, about a mile south of the new(er) Mile High Stadium where the Denver Broncos NFL Franchise has played home games since 2001. The area, once featuring only an extensive subsidized public housing development, now has a small youth center, an early learning center and a remodeled, near state-of-the-art Rude Recreation Center with year-round lunchtime meal service and snacks, a full gymnasium, an indoor pool, a gaming area, weight rooms (with views of Mile High Stadium while you lift!), and an outdoor natural grass baseball diamond and grounds. Longtime residents of the area do fear gentrification and the rising rents that often come with it as they've seen happen in other areas of the city they call home. That would be a shame. Most official head counts of the area show it is made up of approximately 54% children.

Pre-Covid-19 in 2020, the area was not only a beacon for high rise housing developers; it was also the frequent target of recreational developers. Light rail runs through the area, linking it, its recreation opportunities like those at Rude, its children's museum, and its aquarium to the rest of downtown Denver.

Will the developers return? Some in Sun Valley hope so, some do not. Time will tell.

PLEASE LEAVE A REVIEW

If you've enjoyed this book, please tell your friends about it. Did you know that you can lend the book? To do so, simply follow the instructions Amazon provides for loaning a book. Meanwhile, if you have a chance, I would really appreciate an honest review on Amazon. You can review this book by following this link: Misfit Christmas. Thank you!

ABOUT THE AUTHOR

Anne Hagan is the author of more than twenty works of fiction in the mystery, romance, and thriller genres. She writes of family, friends, love, murder, and mayhem in no particular order and often all in the same story. She's a half owner of the weekly discount eBook newsletter, MyLesfic, a wife, parent, foster parent, and an Army veteran. She draws from all of those experiences when she writes because truth is often stranger than fiction.

CHECK ANNE OUT ON HER BLOG, ON FACEBOOK OR ON TWITTER:

For the latest information about upcoming releases, other projects, sample chapters and everything personal, check out Anne's **blog** at https://AnneHaganAuthor.com/ or like Anne on **Facebook** at https://www.facebook.com/AuthorAnneHagan. You can also connect with Anne on **Twitter** @AuthorAnneHagan.

JOIN ANNE'S EMAIL LIST

Are you interested in **free books**? How about **free short stories**? For those and all the latest news on new releases, **opportunities to get review copies of all of her new releases** and more, please consider joining Anne's email list at: https://www.AnneHagan-Author.com by filling in the pop up or using the brief form in the sidebar.

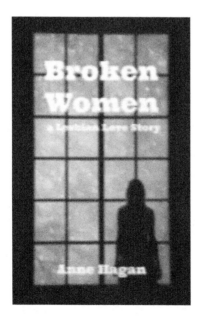

Broken Women

Can two women, unlucky in love, find solace in each other?

Where do you go when you lose everything? Who do you turn to next when nobody seems to want you for more than a casual fling?

When death unexpectedly takes the love of your life, the best you can do is to try to cope and to hold on to the good memories. When your beloved's family takes everything else you have, hope is all that's left... if you can hang on to that.

You've been smitten more than once. You've even been in love a time or two. The trouble is, your feelings are always only yours. Cupid's arrow always fails to land.

Can two love weary people from different worlds find strength together? Can they find more and even a happily ever after?

Healing Embrace–The stand-alone sequel to <u>Broken Women</u>

Barb and Janet were a couple... and then they weren't. What now?

They started a tentative relationship that led to sex a little too soon. Both shied away, but their friends knew the two women belonged together. They conspired to put them together in a neutral place where they could talk it out, and it worked.

They talked. They started slow, with actually dating the second time around... but now what? They've both been shattered by love lost. They're both wary of getting deeply involved again. It doesn't help matters when Barb's focus gets drawn away from her own happiness to tend to others' needs.

Janet tries to be understanding of Barb's need to be there for her family. She knows she loves the fiercely independent blonde, but she's not so sure they belong together in a committed, long-term sort of way, especially when her attempts to lend a hand from time to time seem to bring out more ire than gratefulness.

Barb's dad and his health problems have her feeling years older than she already is. When she looks at the only slightly younger Janet, she sees the exuberance and inexperience of youth. She loves the curvy cop with her heart on her sleeve, but she's afraid the younger woman too often leaps before considering all the consequences.

What will it take to convince the two women that their personalities complement each other and that they're a good match?

Steamboat Reunion–the third and final book in the Barb and Janet series

Can you go home again?

Barb knows she loves Janet, but she's not sure she's ready to take the next step and commit for life. Not again, not so soon. No one is saying it, but she knows they're all thinking she should just move on.

Janet is in love with being in love, and Barb is the object of her affection and devotion. She won't stop until they're married. Oh, she'll be patient, or so she tells everyone who will listen. She'll wait. How long will she have to, though, she wonders?

Just when the two of them start to work things out, Janet is injured on the job, and an old high school crush of Barb's comes back into the picture, a crush who wants things to be the way they were, twenty years before. Both things send Barb into a tailspin of regret and old memories.

Loving Blue in Red States

A lesfic romance ***short story*** series that kicks off with a visit to the little town of Sweetwater, Texas. It's followed by stops in Birmingham, Alabama, Jackson Hole, Wyoming, Perryville, Missouri, Salt Lake City, Utah, Savannah, Georgia, Wall, South Dakota and East Tennessee. More stories will follow for as long as there are 'Red States' in the United States. There's also an international contribution to the series, Kilbirnie Scotland authored by Kitty McIntosh.

A Sweetwater Christmas

Traditional and progressive meet in ruby red west-central Texas...

Emmie Warren is a middle school teacher who is trying not to rock the boat until she can finish her Master's Degree and find the courage to move herself and her son away from sleepy Sweetwater to diverse, vibrant Austin, the only place in Texas she ever felt free to be herself. She's been hiding her truth for years. She doesn't see any reason to change that before making a clean break of things and starting all over.

Cass Prater is a brash cowgirl who lives life out loud wherever she lives. She's got a plan, and she plans to execute it. She's not going to let anything stop her. Cass clashes with Emmie the minute they meet. It's a battle of wills from there on. She's determined to show Emmie she can have it all: her family, a mate, and a job that she loves, right there, in the heart of Texas.

This novella is a significant expansion of the short story, <u>Loving Blue in Red States: Sweetwater Texas</u>.

<u>Christmas Cakes and Kisses</u>

Two different worlds brought together by cake...

When Hannah Yoder left the Amish order at 17, she didn't know what life had in store for her. She just knew she wanted to be free to be herself. Four years later, with the support of a loving family of choice, an adopted son entering full-on toddlerhood, and a new bakery starting to do well, she felt like she had almost everything. Almost. After a previous relationship fizzled out over different life goals, she decided to focus on her son, her business, and completing culinary school before giving any more thought to finding someone new to share her life with.

Morgan Barber has secrets. She hopes culinary school will be her ticket out of the life she hides from the world, a life she wants so desperately to leave behind. With her home life a constant nightmare, a career in chef's whites seems like a beautiful dream. She doesn't dare dream of anything beyond that for herself.

Assigned to work on a Christmas cake baking project together, the two young women are reluctant at first, but they begin to form a bond. Just when Hannah thinks she may have found a spark of the one thing missing in her life, that maybe she can have a relationship with Morgan, the other woman draws away and contemplates changing course entirely.

Can they come together and find joy in the season of joy?

This is a sweet romance featuring a character from Anne's popular Morelville Mysteries series. The book stands alone.

The books of the Morelville Mysteries series; Anne's lesfic themed mystery/romance series:

Relic: The Morelville Mysteries–Book 1–The first Dana and Sheriff Mel mystery and the first book in the Morelville saga. Please click the link above, which will take you to Anne's site, where you can obtain links to get this book.

Cases collide for two star crossed ladies of law enforcement...

Customs Special Agent Dana Rossi was forced to start her life anew after a bad breakup with her former girlfriend and the loss of a job that she loved. These days, she spends life on the road, moving from one case to another until one day when runs run right into the path of Sheriff Mel Crane. The feisty, sexy butch cop is as determined to uncover a counterfeiting ring in her county as Agent Rossi becomes to stop a stalker obsessed with Mel and hot for her company. Dana is under the added pressure of conducting an undercover investigation of her own with a tight deadline: finding and then stopping a ring of smugglers bringing high-end designer knock-offs into the states.

Could their cases be related? When repeated vicious attacks on Mel and her home accelerate the danger for her and their attraction to each other, they become desperate to find the truth and solve the two mysteries. Can they find a way to work together to resolve both cases while coming to terms with their growing feelings for one another? Can Dana move beyond her jilted lover past and find true happiness with a small-town Sheriff?

Busy Bees: The Morelville Mysteries–Book 2

Romance and Murder Mix in the Latest Story Featuring Sheriff Mel Crane and Special Agent Dana Rossi!

Customs Special Agent Dana Rossi is down but not out after being shot and seriously injured during her previous assignment. Will romance blossom, or will sparks fly when she agrees to shack up in Morelville with the beautiful butch Sheriff Melissa 'Mel' Crane and her extended family while she recovers?

Will murder get in the way of love? If murder doesn't, will life in a house with children or a political campaign keep them apart? Can Mel solve two major crimes and keep her former job on the road loving girlfriend happy in a tiny town?

Dana's Dilemma: The Morelville Mysteries–Book 3–The relationship matures between Mel and Dana in an installment that features a breaking Amish character, an ex-girlfriend, a conniving politician, and murder.

Elections and Old Loves Combine with Deadly Results in a Romantic Mystery Featuring Sheriff Mel Crane and Special Agent Dana Rossi!

What happens when Mel runs for Sheriff, an Amish girl runs away from home, and Dana runs–er, limps - for cover? Can anything else possibly go wrong for these two ladies of law enforcement? Sure it can, and it will!

Can the two sometimes lovers work it all out once and for all and finally have a happy life together, or will more crime, murder, and mayhem get in the way?

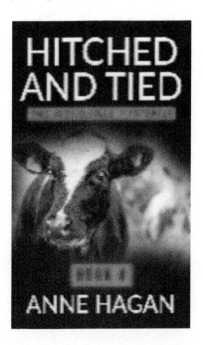

Hitched and Tied: The Morelville Mysteries–Book 4

Mel and Dana attempt to bring their growing romantic relationship full circle, but family, duty, and family duties all conspire to get in the way.

A victim with close ties to the Cranes escapes a deadly assault with his life only to die from his injuries minutes later. Mel has few clues to find the fighter turned murderer, and the further she goes with her investigation, the more the situation deteriorates. Meanwhile, Dana tries to plan their wedding, but the family is resisting both her efforts and the couple's wishes while focusing more on her sister and her traditional relationship.

Family angst, violent crime, and more than a few Holstein steers abound as Dana and Mel fight against the odds to solve Mel's case and find their own happily ever after.

A delayed honeymoon getaway takes a deadly turn for newly-weds Mel and Dana; meanwhile, two meddling mothers won't let sleeping fisherman lie in the latest Morelville Mystery.

Does an unsolved shooting death far away from Morelville have local ties? Did a fisherman really drown, or was there something more sinister afloat?

All Mel and Dana wanted was to enjoy a nice, relaxing honeymoon in the Smokey Mountains, away from the strains of life in the public eye. Instead, they end up involved in a case local law enforcement has completely written off. Things are no better back home where their own mothers are stirring up an all-new hornets' nest that they think Mel and her own department have written off.

If there is going to be any rest for anyone, something will have to break in one case or the other...

A Crane Christmas: The Morelville Mysteries–Book 6

Is it the Christmas season or the 'silly season'?

All Sheriff Mel wants to do is close out the year and spend a joyful first Christmas with Dana and their extended families. She's even hired a new detective, Janet Mason, to ease some of the workload for her and her only other detective, Shane Harding. Things were shaping up great for her and Dana for a relaxing holiday season. Too bad it just wasn't meant to be...

The local criminals want it all too, and a string of burglaries in high-class county enclaves has Mel and both of her detectives stymied. Throw in a bunch of disappearing dogs, some designer sheep, a lonely woman, and an unsolved murder case, and the good guys are at their wits' end. Meanwhile, back in tiny little

Morelville, things aren't much better; the village is buzzing over Dana's family taking over the store, but Dana herself isn't so sure that's a good thing.

Can Mel and her team resolve everything before Christmas dinner comes out of the oven? Will Janet Mason fit in at all? Will Dana find a balance between work and family that works for her in time to enjoy her first Christmas with Mel?

Mad for Mel: The Morelville Mysteries–Book 7

Rival gangs will stop at nothing to gain sole control of the drug trade in Muskingum County, and they've picked Valentine's week to create a firestorm of murder and mayhem as they battle each other for supremacy.

Sheriff Mel Crane is blindsided by looting, murdering, and marauding bikers at a time of year when most Harley's are tucked safely away from the effects of Ohio winters that come rife with snow and ice. They're rolling out, they're out of control, and she can't stop them. On the home front, she's feeling guilty about spending so much time working and hardly any time with Dana, especially when she knows Valentine's Day is right around the corner... or so her mother-in-law keeps reminding her.

Dana just wants Mel to be safe; she has her own problems to worry about. Her attempt at novel writing isn't going as well as she hoped, and she's bored. She got a little taste of what it was like to be an investigator again, and she misses it. What to do?

Hannah's Hope: The Morelville Mysteries–Book 8

A young mother with a troubled past seeks help from Mel and Dana, but is their effort to assist her too little, too late?

Hannah Yoder appears on Dana and Mel's doorstep late one night with her teenage friend Katie and Katie's newborn baby in tow, telling the couple the girl and child are in trouble and have no place else to go. Dana and Mel offer refuge for the night and a firm promise to talk about the future. Plans are barely made when first one mysterious tragedy strikes and then another leaving Mel, Dana, Hannah, and the Crane and Rossi families with few clues and little hope.

Mel knows there's a killer out there; she just doesn't know where to start looking. She's stonewalled at every turn and running out of time. Somebody knows something that will unlock the mysteries swirling all around, but who?

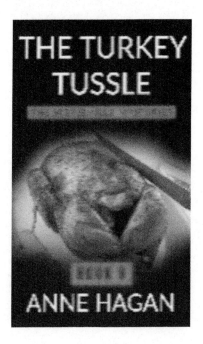

The Turkey Tussle: The Morelville Mysteries–Book 9

The old-fashioned country village of Morelville holds a secret.

Faye Crane has the perfect life as a homemaker, farmer's wife, and grandmother... or she did until her daughter-in-law Dana went and stirred up a mysterious murder, never resolved and long-buried in the Lafferty family lore–before Faye ever became a Crane. Now she's been reminded of some startling questions about her family's past that she's not sure she wants to know the answers to.

Dana knows to tread lightly around Faye. Their relationship is far from perfect, but she just can't help herself; she's certainly intrigued by the unsolved case. The down to earth, gentle residents of the village are more than happy to fill her in on all the old gossip too. She even gets an education in oil drilling and backroom poker along her way to trying to clear the Lafferty family name and bring some closure to her mother-in-law. The question is, can she figure it all out and, if she does, will the Lafferty's and the Crane's be better off or far worse?

Sullied Sally: The Morelville Mysteries–Book 10

An unsolved murder, more than 40 years in the past, leads to the discovery of a new victim and the return of an old stalker.

After a blow to the head, Owen Lafferty lay dying, alone in a cabin, far out in the woods and far from home. He was found by Dana Rossi-Crane as she happened along, chasing around the threads of a 1972 unsolved murder involving her mother-in-law, Faye, and Owen and his family. Dana's efforts were, unfortunately, too little, too late to save Owen.

With the two murders 40 some years apart, looking like they're related, a cast of suspects now in their sixties and seventies and very set in their ways, and a wife who won't stay out of her cases, Sheriff Mel Crane already has her hands full. A new Deputy

District Attorney coming in and horning in on her investigation and her old stalker's return don't help matters.

Can Mel solve either case? Can she convince the new Deputy DA that she's not hiding evidence to protect her family? Is Sally's reason for showing back up in Mel's life legitimate or a ruse to get close to her again? Will Dana butt out? Stay tuned!

Finding Sheila: The Morelville Mysteries–Book 11

A woman, imprisoned for manslaughter, disappears without a trace during transport between states, and it's all up to Dana to find her.

Sheila Ford traveled to Tennessee, planning to commit an act of premeditated murder on her husband. Her lone shot at him misses and kills his lover instead. After pleading guilty to a manslaughter charge, she's locked away in a Tennessee prison for women. Everyone back home in Ohio wrote her off. She wasn't eligible for a parole hearing for seven years.

When Jennifer Coventry calls begging Sheriff Mel Crane to bring her ailing mother home to Ohio to serve out the rest of her sentence in the county jail, close to home, Mel is reluctant but gives in. The only problem is, she's so short-staffed and can't send a deputy to do the transport. She deputizes Dana to do the duties.

Dana planned to go to Tennessee anyway, to look at a vacation cabin for herself and Mel. A little detour over to Nashville to connect with Sheila and the ambulance transporting her to Ohio won't be hard, she thought... until everything that could go wrong does, ending up with Sheila disappearing during a rest stop.

A multi-state search is on to find the escaped convict and return her to prison, but the circumstances of her disappearance go far deeper than anyone could have imagined.

Tennessee Bound: The Morelville Mysteries–Book 12

The politics and the paper-pushing are wearing on Sheriff Mel. Will she chuck it all?

Mel's burned out. She's tired of playing local politics. She's tired of the mounds of paper on her desk that never seem to diminish. She's tired of budgets, personnel conflicts, citizen complaints, and all the other things a sheriff is responsible for. She misses police work. Real police work, but she knows she can't go back to the street. Not in Muskingum County... maybe not in Ohio.

Dana bought a cabin–a nice little getaway for the two of them in Tennessee. Mel's mom is worried her daughter will fly the family coop and roost in Tennessee full time; maybe she'll even take a street cop job there.

Dana and Mel head to Tennessee to see their new home

away from home, take a breather from work and family, and talk about the future. Mel's future. Their future. Mel has some surprises for Dana, but her thoughts on stepping down as Sheriff and where she's thinking about going next take a backseat to what happens during their getaway.

A spinoff from the Morelville Mysteries series, The Morelville Cozies series feature meddling mother sleuths Faye Crane and Chloe Rossi getting mixed up in mysteries all their own.

The Passed Prop: The Morelville Cozies–Book 1

Chloe Rossi wants to retire with her husband and move away from suburban sprawl to bucolic Morelville; the only trouble is, Morelville is experiencing its worst crime wave ever, and Marco Rossi wants no part of a move there. What to do?

Faye Crane would like nothing more than to have her good friend Chloe move closer to her and to Chloe's own daughter. She's got Chloe convinced it's a smart move, but Marco is a tougher nut to crack. A string of brutal crimes around Halloween with no witnesses and little evidence to work with has her own Sheriff daughter and her entire department stymied. Marco is second-guessing even taking his retirement since Sheriff Mel can't get a handle on it all and bring peace and well-being back to the tiny village.

Someone has to root out a killer. Can Faye and Chloe nose around and figure out what the police can't to solve the crime? If they do, will Marco still waver, or will he consent to move?

Opera House Ops: The Morelville Cozies–Book 2

Murder and other sinister goings-on at a vacant 1800s era opera house in Morelville and a modern-day property developer who wants to raze the historic building for his own gain have the village residents all tied up in knots and Faye Crane trying to play savior to history.

Faye Crane and Chloe Rossi are back in a second Morelville cozy mystery. This time, sinister goings-on, including the discovery of a dead body at a vacant late 1800s era opera house in Morelville, have the village residents all tied up in knots. When what first appears to be an accident turns out to be murder, the duo of meddling mothers quickly gets enmeshed in another round of crime-solving. It doesn't help that, everywhere they turn, a property hungry developer with more money than sense wants the land the building sits on, and he'll seemingly stop at nothing to get it.

Is there really another killer in their midst? Is the same person responsible for all the strange occurrences? What will it take to make the crimes stop, make a developer go away, and save the historic building for future generations?

Three multi-eBook boxed sets of the Morelville Mysteries works by Anne Hagan are also available for purchase.

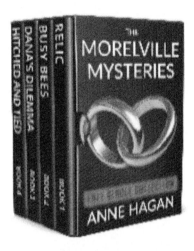

The Morelville Mysteries Full Circle Collection is a five eBook set that contains the first four Morelville Mysteries novels and an exclusive <u>Companion Guide</u> that is only available with this set.

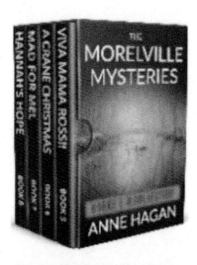

The Morelville Mysteries: Books 5-8 Collection

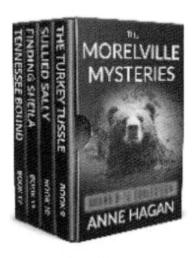

The Morelville Mysteries: Books 9-12 Collection

~

Steel City Confidential–Anne's first legal thriller

Clients hide things from their lawyers all the time. Pam Wilson makes it an art form.

Pam's been on the run from the law for years, and she was getting away with it. The statute of limitations ran out on most of her crimes. For her spouse Charlotte? Not so much. Though they were aging, they looked forward to enjoying their golden years and, hopefully, forgetting about the past.

Life got complicated when Charlotte became gravely ill, their daughter got pregnant with the child of a married man... a married man someone took shots at from a rare motorcycle Pam happens to own. When the man was shot again and killed in his office at Pitt a couple of weeks later, the police found all signs pointing to Pam.

Rochelle 'Ro' Rabinowitz, a second-generation Pittsburgh lawyer, and her little firm take on Pam's case pro-bono. Ro thinks it's a slam dunk for the defense and hands the case off to her new associate and–she hopes–her future partner in the firm, Dominique, to get her feet wet in a courtroom. Clients are never completely honest with their lawyers, and Ro and Dominque soon learn this one is no exception.

Slam dunk? More like a pipe dream...

Printed in Great Britain
by Amazon